# SWIMMING THE CHANNEL

# SWIMMING
# THE CHANNEL

## Jill Neville

St. Martin's Press
New York

Library of Congress Cataloging-in-Publication Data

Neville, Jill.
Swimming the channel / Jill Neville.
p.    cm.
"A Thomas Dunne book."
ISBN 0-312-11337-4
1. Married people—Great Britain—Fiction.   2. Teenage
girls—Great Britain—Fiction.   3. Diplomats—Great Britain—
Fiction.   4. British—France—Paris—Fiction.   I. Title.
PR9619.3.N45S95   1994
823—dc20   94-31314   CIP

First published in Great Britain by Bloomsbury Publishing Ltd.

First U.S. Edition: December 1994
10  9  8  7  6  5  4  3  2  1

To Lewis

*C. VAUGHN-FURR*
*2000*

# BETH

## 1969

*Ce n'est plus une ardeur dans mes veines cachée:*
*C'est Vénus toute entière à sa proie attachée.*

Racine, Phèdre

# ONE

A white cat came into a winter garden. It was raining, but not too heavily, and the London sky was the usual consistency of porridge. The cat streaked up a tree, eyes yellowing in the dusk, aware of a blob of darkness to be avoided, like the larger, noisier blobs that showed absolutely no mercy on the road.

The man walking along with a hint of a swagger was also watched by a street sweeper. It was the end of the year but not yet time for Christmas. Paul thought of the fuss his mother would make, the long conversations about decorations in her Sussex house, gifts for people in whom he had no interest, her spindly tables and inlaid escritoire gleaming under holly arrangements, hurting his eyes like powdered glass.

He recognized some of his mother's hectic fussiness in himself. But at this point in his life he is trying to lunge in the opposite direction, which is one of the reasons he has committed himself to do some blistering articles for Tom Scrutton's newspaper.

The communal gardens were curved; they had once been part of a racecourse. Between the fences, hedges dripped. The cat shot out before him, rushing ahead like a demented fate. He pondered on the subterranean life of cats in communal gardens and wondered if a sociologist had got on to it.

A few doors along, in Tom Scrutton's living room, his wife Beth was sitting with her feet curled underneath her on the sofa in a sea of the previous week's newspapers. She wore a white crêpe blouse, rather loose (one shoulder *would* keep slipping down), a grey wool skirt with a wine stain on the front, and she had her shoes off.

Tom was talking shop. He had to oust someone from the newsroom who would not be dislodged by mere neglect or subtle humiliation, so something bolder had to be devised, short of actually firing him, because that would cause too much ɩf a commotion. Tom was one of the senior editors of the newspaper known for taking the underdog's side. To fire an old-timer would provoke sniggers in *Private Eye*. They weren't in a recession, when lay-offs were recognized to be unavoidable.

'Perhaps you could send him abroad somewhere, like Djakarta?' she suggested vaguely, not knowing a thing about the place, but aware that was what they usually did in this situation.

The front doorbell rang. 'Ah, that'll be Paul Radcliffe,' said Tom, and chuckled. He had reeled in a star. Still in his socks, he opened the door. (His shoes, and Beth's, were drying by the fire.)

The young diplomat entered the hall, taking off his coat, and glimpsing at the same time his reflection in a mirror, he noticed with alarm that it was one of those nights when he looked repellently gilded, like a descending, priapic god. His too-good looks had always been an embarrassment. Not everyone trusted him in the Civil Service, for it was believed that the gods, giving with one hand, must surely take away with the other.

As he entered the living room of the man he was about to cuckold he was struck by a gust of warmth and a delightful sense of negligence. Beth, one shoulder of her blouse still

4

dropping, leaned forward on the sofa to shake his hand, newspapers crackling beneath her haunches.

'Ah, Paul Radcliffe, the diplomat who wants to sell his soul to the printer's devil.'

'Inside every toff there's a tart.'

She gave him her cascading smile; her glowing messiness seducing him at once. He had never met a woman so alert yet so relaxed, as if the whole universe were her bower and around her head little zephyrs blew (cherubs holding gauze over her private parts, possibly the fruit of her womb, or mere metaphorical babies).

Childbirth hadn't aged her, or given her that fixed look of perpetual vigilance. She had once had that look, as a matter of fact, when her babies were lurching about the house on a level with electric plugs, but now that they were all in some form of higher education she had reverted to the person her husband had adored at school: the mischief-maker, the applauder, the egger-on, the boy's girl.

But Tom no longer wished to make love to her. There were limits, weren't there, as to how long one could take the same path through the woods and find new delights.

'Paul's going to do us a tough political series, sweetheart, when he can sneak the time. It'll be a new young voice, from the establishment; the heart of darkness.'

'You mean lightness, surely,' teased Paul.

'Everyone knows what attitude Tom's paper will take about everything,' said Beth, pulling the blouse up on her shoulder, feeling naked all of a sudden under the gaze of the new protégé.

When the newspaper had managed to get Paul to sign a six-month contract to do a weekly piece Tom had been so pleased. A star, he chortled. We needed a star. They had tried editorship by committee and the no-star system – all commendably democratic – but the paper grew so dull the circulation had dropped.

'I'll try to surprise you,' Paul said, tearing his eyes away from Beth to his employer.

'Not by being too Blimpish. Don't want to scare off the young idealists. The circulation's soared since the Vietnam war.'

'But won't you have to be very cautious not to offend your masters in the corridors of power?' Beth asked, finding the weave in her old skirt intensely compelling.

'I could resort to a pseudonym.' Paul began to air his views on the American intervention in Vietnam and other topics that were even more hazardous for an ambitious diplomat but which he would handle with cunning.

Every now and then Tom put more coal on the fire; strictly illegal in a smokeless zone, but so far they'd got away with it. When there was no more coal in the scuttle he threw on a log which hissed and filled the room with a smell of pine. A line from the Song of Songs came into Paul's mind as he was in mid-analysis of the killing fields: '*Also our bed is green. The beams of our house are cedar and our rafters of fir.*' To be in a green bed with such a woman as Beth, knowing you had built the rafters of fir and the beams of cedar – how *earthed* one would feel. And there would be a fire in the bedroom, a real fire; the light would be off and the woman's body would be lit all over by firelight, feathered in it, as her face was at this moment.

In fact the flush under Beth's skin was partly caused by drink and firelight and partly by her natural Welsh heritage. Given a bad time, bad luck and poverty she could have been a very plain woman, like her female ancestors, with something of the turnip about that squatness and endurance, unenlivened by flame or fun. She had been brought up with lots of brothers, all sleeping in a heap under their father's army greatcoat. She had escaped via the local grammar school, but still retained a Welsh belief in magic, seeming encased in some bubble of shining optimism. Her night dreads were kept strictly under wraps, between herself and her pillow; not even Tom latched on to the full extent of this harrowing counterpoint to her merry-seeming life.

A cat pushed the door open with its nose and rushed into the room, straight towards where Beth sat, jumping on to the sofa and scratching at it frenziedly, tearing it to shreds.

'He's mad, that cat. He's Welsh. Got to be.' She picked him up but he jumped crazily on to her shoulders, so she shoved him off again, but too late, for he had clawed her cheek. In disgrace, he contented himself with scraping his claws on the leg of the sofa, ruining the polish and the wood, but no one seemed to mind. It would indeed be hard to imagine Beth in a room of spiky edges, where consciousness of the polish of wood rode uppermost in her mind.

Outside, the street sweeper stuffed leaves into a hessian bag. He stood and rested for a while, leaning on his witch's broom, looking in at the brilliant room where a woman lay on a sofa talking to two men. One man was showing signs of booze; the other was a smooth bastard. He was staring at the woman, who looked a bit of a tart.

Beth hardly moved all evening. Tom did all the drink and food serving (on the coffee table, with no napkins). He also led the conversation. She provided enough by just existing, it seemed. Tom chain-smoked, coughed, drank, got red in the face, laughed at his own jokes. He was Lunch-Time O'Booze in person, but with an unusual toughness at centre. Paul seemed grim by comparison, with something feline and stealthy about him. He drank slowly, ate slowly, told stories about chaps in high places; goaded on to enter perilous waters, but always stopping this side of indiscretion.

He looked at his watch and exclaimed at the lateness of

the hour. In the rush of departure, or the rush of some semi-conscious strategy, he left his notebook behind, in which he had jotted down some of the ideas that had emerged over dinner.

The following morning, after Tom left for the newspaper, Beth found it among the debris. She opened the crocodile-skin cover and saw Paul's address and telephone numbers clearly inscribed in case of loss. In some ways Paul was very like his mother.

She phoned him at his flat the next evening, at the time when she was always at her most lonely, when she felt the absence of the children and the absence of Tom, who would undoubtedly be drinking and flirting with cronies in Fleet Street. She phoned Paul then, holding her second glass of wine to give her courage, willing her hand to stop shaking and her voice to sound calm and normal; wondering if she wasn't too old for the game.

She arrived at Paul's Chelsea address bearing the notebook and a bottle of wine. Her perceptions seemed weird, distorted. A red mailbox loomed out of the dusk. She walked up the steps: one, two, three, four, avoiding the cracks like a child. He had to come down three flights to open the door, and when she saw him she was struck by the gaiety in his face. He must have known it was all an excuse to see him again; that his ruse had worked. She could have sent him the notebook, popped it in the post, and that would have been the end of the whole thing.

His flat was anonymous: painted white throughout and with cautiously-coloured drapes and furnishings, not unlike a business motel. He had made little effort to imprint his personality on his surroundings, except for one nice rug. There were no photographs of mothers, fathers, grandmothers, dogs. There were no paintings or prints or bric-à-brac. Even the crockery was standard stuff, and the glasses the kind you could hire and break. There was no cosiness to hide behind; no camp fire they could sit around and throw distracting screens of talk between themselves and their blatant desires.

But Beth chose to sit in the rocking chair: the single piece of furniture that looked as if it came from somewhere else, another life; where there had been some kind of social history, tender memories. She sat in the rocker but kept her coat buttoned as if under interrogation.

'I must be disturbing your work,' she said, looking at papers piled on the table.

'I was just doing my accounts,' he called. He was in the tiny kitchen, pouring drinks. 'I don't bring my work home.'

She felt that a brick of some kind had got lodged in her chest so that, around it, whatever oxygen she managed to inhale had to struggle its way through. She longed suddenly for a bath – her own bathroom lined with photographs and pictures and decorated Pompeii red; the whole thing to be safely over so that she could think about it afterwards.

Paul walked towards her, holding a glass of champagne. She sat hunched up in his wicker rocking chair that had once been in his father's study and had talismanic power. He placed the drink on the table, pulled her up by her upper arms (which he had been longing to touch ever since the drooping-blouse evening), hauled her in to a very long kiss. One of those ones that feel right: the lips not too wet or dry, the pressure not too hard or soft, and an all invasive source of heat. They locked hands, pushing at each other's palms as if trying to exchange fingerprints. He pulled her curls back from her forehead and squinted at her as if through glare coming off bright water. Her hands moved over him, her fingers slid into his mouth, and he sucked dreamily, staring at her through the dazzle, obsessed by the cat's scratch-marks on her cheek. Always before, Paul had had to steer things, a bit

9

like driving dodgems; always it reminded him of that Cole Porter song about the faint aroma of performing seals. But this was not performing seals. Things were occurring with their own inner velocity. Shadows from the street wound through their bodies. Headlights slid along the darkening wall. Furniture tumbled over. During their most violent moment the telephone rang until Paul kicked the receiver off and it went dead.

When she lay basking on the carpet, her hand under her head, he handed her the still volatile champagne. Drinking it was to have been the first stage of seduction, but they had had as much time for seduction as a chip of iron hurtling towards a magnet.

'What time do your children get back from school?' he asked in a changed voice; the crisp edges had melted.

She took the filled glass, splashing a little on the carpet. Despite himself, his triumphant animal self, a tiny worry registered itself in Paul's pernickety mind. That carpet was Persian and very old indeed; so old it had a silver patina. She swallowed the champagne. 'My children are quite grown-up.'

'You must have had them when you were a child yourself.'

'Well, Tom and I were school sweethearts.' She would not tell him how old she was. Not yet. It would ruin the atmosphere.

Paul picked up the rug and studied the very faint champagne mark. You would have to be down there on all fours and with a magnifying glass to notice it when it dried. But when she left he would sponge it. No, he was not so very unlike his prudent mother as he liked to believe. But they would lie on it again, those two, during the next few weeks, many times. He knew that already.

# TWO

B eth suggested they meet where no one would find them: at the tea-room of the crematorium at Golders Green. He had laughed at her joke, being of an age when friends seldom drop dead.

Beth arrived first, which didn't worry her. With Paul it would simply be a matter of traffic jams: no sudden changes of heart; no unsuspected rivals. It was pleasant to feel so securely adored.

At first she couldn't find the place and wondered if, while attending the last in a stream of recent cremations, she had imagined it. But no, there it was tucked in the corner of the quadrangle, out of sight. She entered its muted primness and sat by the window, touching the flowers in the vase, real violets.

An aged waitress in apple-green came over.

'I'm waiting for someone. We'll just be wanting a pot of tea, I think.' Then, arms on the table, she stared out at the wintry trees. Below them, bright bunches of florist flowers covered neat squares which, she presumed, contained ashes of the departed. Shafts of winter light moved over rose bushes which displayed the occasional stoic bloom. Despite the gloom of it, Beth was ridiculously happy; the kind that can't last, because nothing is better than it.

11

Somehow it had not been very pleasant over the last years, watching Tom succumb to the Spirit of the Times; and although he wasn't furtive about it, and she tried to be brave and insouciant and do likewise, her heart wasn't in it. How she wished he *would* be furtive about it. But no, he announced he was going out again with one of his blondes, so young, so discouragingly slender, leaving her with some man whose attentions she had dutifully encouraged, just to make Tom happy, really, so he wouldn't feel guilty at leaving Cinderella behind. (Anyway, when had guilt become something dirty, something to be shunned at all costs?) But usually she would get rid of the man far too early, before he struck the definitive blow. She needed to feel passion, but Tom said that never happened to him and that it was exceedingly dangerous.

It didn't feel particularly dangerous. It felt like swimming that time, in Paphos. Tom had taken her to Cyprus and, for fun, she dipped into the icy pool said to be the birthplace of Aphrodite (half covered in Cypriot litter). The sea was also said to be the birthplace of Aphrodite, so she swam there too, right across the bay towards a huge white rock. It had felt like flying, because the water was so buoyant; the amniotic fluid for the goddess of love, beauty and anarchy.

It was buoyancy she felt now, in this rebirth. She knew people at Tom's office thought Paul was an arrogant bastard. But that was envy, of course. Paul glittered. It wasn't just because everyone knew about his academic honours; it wasn't just his excessive good looks, his family wealth, his luck; he was fun as well, and most wonderful of all he was honest: a good egg.

The door opened, and Beth looked up in sparkling readiness to meet her lover, but a drab woman peeped in. She disappeared for a moment, then pushed in a disabled man, in a wheelchair. When she turned the chair around, the man in the chair looked at Beth and winked. Beth smiled, then turned back to study the garden of death.

How had the poor sod become wheelchair bound? Was it one of those endless ailments that Tom had a special team to investigate and write about in harrowing detail (almost every day it seemed)? Over the years she had learned to protect herself from the constant nag of empathy. At Christmas time the charities became too much, cancelling each other out, and she resented being accused of complacency if she went for a while without worrying about the slings and arrows of other people's outrageous fortune. Sometimes she pulled down the portcullis on all compassion, walking brutally away from beggars. One cunning desperado at the Tottenham Court Road tube station watched out for her now and spat.

'No, Stanley, you don't want that cake. It'll get all over you and then I'll have to wash that shirt again.' The woman took an éclair out of her husband's shaking hand, wiping his chin bossily.

That man's manhood was being squashed more by the woman than by the wheelchair. And he was so brawny. The lustrousness of his hair so virile. How she would have liked to unlock Samson's chains, see him rise up, strike down the hag and stalk off, bearing a holly club, into the forest where he belonged. Hadn't that always been her role? With Tom she had been the maenad attending Dionysus as she spat grape-pips into the wind.

Tom and she had been like that from the start, even at school; she egging him on. And it had been a good marriage when the children were small. It was just journalism. Since Tom had become an editor all the little bitches had hurled themselves at him. He couldn't have enough. While they spouted sisterly love, they trampled over each other to mate with the cock of the walk. Even in front of Beth they stared at

Tom like hypnotists, as if she, Beth, were invisible; or stuck, like that man in a wheelchair, in a sexless trap.

But now of course Tom's cavortings turned out to be a blessing. She didn't have to feel guilty. She was going to let Tom know what was going on, very soon. But somehow she kept putting it off. For once she didn't feel like dissecting a relationship. What occurred between herself and Paul was private. It was Tom who was the outsider now. It was her relationship with Tom that was discussed in the high and creaking bed, at home in the afternoons, or on the divan at Paul's little flat. Discussed with Paul and dissected.

Paul arrived, only five minutes late, with snow on his lapels; yes, snow had just started to fall, lolling down sideways like almond blossom.

He whispered in her ear, 'Brilliant place for a drop.' A flake of snow fell in her hair. He sat down, letting his coat fall over the back of the chair. 'Adultery is good training for espionage.'

'Not as good, they say, as homosexuality.' The hovering waitress flinched at their banter, but disapproved more of the calm assurance with which the woman glanced at the man. Her eyes skidded along his face like a swan landing on still water.

He picked up her hand and studied the particularity of her fingernails, noticing with delight that they were slightly dirty. 'Well?'

'Let's have tea first.'

He ordered a pot of tea for two. The man in the wheelchair wanted to muscle in; participate in the shine around their bit of the café. 'I'm a cripple . . .'

'Disabled, dear,' corrected his wife.

'I'm a cripple and I want to eat éclairs because that's my only pleasure, but I'm not allowed. You two don't eat cakes because you've got the whole world before you, that's obvious.'

'Stanley!' The woman dropped her handbag on the floor and a lipstick rolled towards them. Beth picked up Revlon's 'Hot Lips' and handed it back to the tight-lipped woman. Stanley sank back to take his medicine. 'Just an accident, during army training up in Wensleydale. We were going over a gully on a rope. I fell. Must have been dreaming. Life's like that. One mistake. One tiny failure and that's it. Lights out. No more freedom. No more fun on the sly, like some. Not even chocolate éclairs.' He surrendered to the pills, which were handed over with some brackish-looking tea to wash them down.

'That's terrible,' Paul said, letting go of Beth's hand, feeling the crudeness of displayed happiness. He had wondered if other people could see that when he looked at Beth it felt as if their faces were fucking. It seemed they could. Paul and Beth stared out at the crematorium. They had been going to arrange a weekend together in Paris, but it seemed hubristic. Her kitschy joke – tea at the crematorium – had rebounded. The only mourners who had come in to the place were half dead themselves. The lovers did not touch each other. Just drank their tea and stared out at more black-coated mourners assembling beyond the trees, laying down wreaths, some sobbing.

Stanley was wheeled out of the room in silence. He had slipped down in his chair sleepily; his wife's blood-red mouth did not open to speak even the word goodbye.

'Darling Beth. You must be able to get away, just for a few days.'

'Well, there's Thursday night.' There was an editorial conference on Thursday night. Tom, of course, ran the show. Then everyone usually went to El Vino's for a drink. That was where various girls insinuated themselves into Tom's life and bed. Yes, of course, Thursday she would be free; but it amazed him that she would tailor her absences to fit Tom's.

'I suppose we could at least fit in a night in Dieppe,' she agreed at last, and he stopped being too greedy, hoping for the impossible, like a whole week in her arms, and imagined at last being with her on the cross-channel ferry; having supper on French soil, making love in a French hotel with wonderful food and a great big French bed, waking to croissants and *deux grandes crèmes*. Better than nothing. He picked up her hand and stroked each finger as if smoothing a glove. Even in this place Eros held sway over Thanatos.

She filled him in on the last twenty-four hours since they met, the antics of acquaintances, and he watched one particular set of muscles on her left cheek contract and decontract. He became randy again, the bull in the tea-shop.

He'd like to take her outside and screw her on all those graves. But it was more than physical. He had knowledge of her essence: her golden, generous, forgiving self; de-toxing all his held-in rancour. Lying against her body was like visiting some long-remembered beach where he had once been happy.

Paul and Beth were at that stage when it had been going on for so long (six and a half weeks) they believed that nothing could now go wrong. Six and a half weeks was just enough time for the matter to be brought to the full attention of the gods, after getting through their considerable bureaucratic pile-up.

# THREE

It was basically an all-male bar, but women were allowed to filter in as long as they lay low and stayed on the fringes of things; as long as they were young and pretty; eyes oiled by hormones and expectation. The junior librarian appeared. She had the regulation long blonde hair, mini-skirt and shoulderbag. The men fell roughly into two categories: Chewed Rope and Cherubs. The Cherubs were belligerent, with bow-lips, pouched eyes and red complexions. They always ended up with heart trouble. Often they failed to hold their liquor, but there was always a dazzling period before they subsided into abuse, self-pity or stupor, when they were fun to have around. At this stage they gave off the warmth and intimacy of golden-hearted tarts.

Tom was a Cherub, but he could hold his liquor. Indeed, his metabolism was the envy of the newsroom. Even during the Six Day War, when he had worked round the clock, his trusty bottle of Scotch at his elbow, Tom had never so much as slurred a word – on paper or in the nubile ear of one of his girls. It was partly this extraordinary gift that had enabled Tom to rise to the heights of editorship. Other, flashier, performers had disgraced themselves in one way or another too often to be offered the crown.

The librarian, Betsy, hovered demurely on the edge of

Tom's circle. She had received the touch of the lion's paw at the office party and was waiting for him to come back for the kill. Except she found it so hard to wait; she had ventured into El Vino's.

'So, did you fire the old hack?' asked Paul, *sotto voce*, gazing in the opposite direction to the subject of his enquiry, who now leaned against the bar in isolation. He was a Chewed Rope; dried out, with a bilious eye and a face frayed with largely futile endeavour and the claw of deadlines.

'Well, no. He filed a brilliant piece yesterday. Brilliant. On draft-dodgers from the US Army. Lots of them are hiding in Paris, you know.'

'Why don't you send him to the States? The Washington office. Isn't Booth retiring soon?'

The librarian finally caught Tom's eye. Her lips parted, and with one hand she swept back her long bedroom hair.

'It's a thought,' murmured Tom, not thinking about it at all, merely working out when he would have time to do something about the librarian. But meanwhile there was something else he had to do. It was a bit ticklish; worse than trying to get rid of the hack at the bar. He had to ask Paul if his intentions towards his wife were honourable. Mad, really, but he couldn't have Beth's heart broken. She was his responsibility. He'd known her since she was 13. She'd smuggled cigarettes to him under the desks. She'd taught him to play the guitar and helped him with his maths. One night they met at midnight on the beach at Pendine and, lying there, listening to all that wind and sea, he'd known she belonged to him for ever. She was always a bit of a madcap, and even when the babies were tiny she was never totally demolished by hormones into the cabbage state.

But now he didn't like the look in her eyes. It was so different from her normal humorous twinkle. When he came home, instead of bombarding him with gossip and questions, she would be sitting in the half-light, staring at the view, and would start with intense surprise when he switched on the light and then scan his face for a moment as if she were trying to recall his name.

It's true he had encouraged her to have lovers – after all, they were both getting on. What was the point of being faithful to each other when the passion thing had evaporated; soon they'd be lying in coffins and worms would try her long-preserved virginity. Well, hardly virginity, but she once said she felt that her virginity had been renewed by many years of marital abstinence.

She didn't blame him, of course; she understood about man the hunter, and the de-sexing effluent of long-term relationships. He'd definitely encouraged her to do likewise: to have flings; to have her equivalent of the librarian; but her heart wasn't in it.

Unfortunately her heart seemed to be rather too much in Paul Radcliffe. And of course that would lead to one thing only; deep distress for his old sweetheart.

No. It wouldn't do. It was a bit difficult. But after just one more drink he'd have to broach the subject.

'Have a drink, Patsy,' he said. The librarian ordered a Babycham, dropping her eyelashes like the gazelle in the advertisement, then lifting them artfully. 'My name's Betsy.'

'I'd better be off,' said Paul, who had dropped in with his fourth piece, but Tom begged him to stay. He had something to discuss. When Paul went to the Gents, Tom whispered something to the girl, who finished her drink. She had gone by the time Paul emerged.

The doomed Chewed Rope was glancing at them as if he might be going to join them. So Tom suggested that he and Paul take a stroll. 'Could be bugged in here. And this is seriously private stuff.'

For the next half-hour they walked up and down Fleet Street, as far down as the *Daily Express* office, which flashed back their distorted, gesticulating reflections; then back up by the Law Courts, then down again, then up again.

'You see, old man, she's my responsibility. I love her dearly. Always will. Can't have her heart broken.'

'There's no danger of that. In fact . . . '

'I know she's in love with you. The real thing.' He laughed softly. 'She always did have good taste. Good taste in everything. Mind you, she's not an angel. Bit untidy round the place. Wonderful mother. Even now that they've grown and flown . . . motherhood is her *métier* . . . she should have run an orphanage. Still, they've gone and I think that's the problem, doesn't know what to do with her emotions.'

'A mother isn't all she is.'

'She's a woman, of course. Of course. I should know. I married her. But . . . ' He had to break off as they dodged across the road, nearly hit by a dispatch rider. 'So I mean, old chap, I think you'd better melt away before it's too late.'

Paul remained silent, then said, in a low but steely voice, 'It's impossible.'

'No, no, no . . . it's not impossible. It just *seems* impossible. I'll send you to Washington, I'll give you a column. All this will just melt away.'

'I don't want to be a full-time journalist, Tom. And you keep using verbs like "melt". But this thing between us is not for the melting. It's unmeltable, I'm telling you. Not like your . . . '

'Oh, that. That's my *joie de vivre*. Love doesn't come into it. Love is a bloody nuisance. And I'm not having you break my wife's heart. I don't intend to spend the rest of my life trying to put back the pieces.'

'I want to marry Beth. I want you and Beth to get a divorce so that we can get married.'

Tom stopped. His entire bulk seemed to totter like a building in the vicinity of an explosion. 'Married? She is married.'

'I know. But you can get unmarried.'

The two men were now at the top of Fleet Street. They crossed the road again, traffic sliced past them on both sides like the blades of an approaching chainsaw. They took refuge beneath the statue of Samuel Johnson: '*Critic, essayist, philologist, biographer, wit, poet, moralist, dramatist, political writer, talker.*' The supreme Cherub. They edged through parked taxis and went into the church of St Clement Danes.

Tom went to the south aisle. Paul peered into cabinets crammed with Church silver, staring long and hard at a christening mug which had once belonged to a Battle of Britain pilot shot down in a dogfight. Tom sat down in the back pew and hung his head as if praying. Paul, who was a fastidious atheist, remembered that Tom had been brought up in Wales and would take to prayer and song with equal enthusiasm.

Paul gazed away at the Pre-Raphaelite angels. His mind cleared. A wonderful calmness rose in him. He would marry Beth and that would be that; love with a capital L.

Tom lifted his head and said, 'You're about 30, aren't you?'

'Twenty-nine.'

'Yes, I thought so. Well Beth is 45, or is it 46?'

Paul sat down in the same pew, but at some distance. He stared at the embroidered prayer cushion on the hook before him. He traced the edge of an embroidered rose with his finger.

'She looks at least fifteen years younger than that, I know, old son. It's her wonderful health and vitality; not a grey hair. Yet.'

The christening mug of the dead pilot shone its beam down on Paul.

Tom started strolling up the aisle. This church didn't have any mystery. No holy feel. It was too official. Too dusted and polished. The trouble with the English when they loved something too much, they tidied it to death; like Winchester Cathedral; like cottages in the Cotswolds. They loved atmosphere. That's why they all raved about little French villages where *clochards* pissed on ancient ruins and then they went there and bought up the place and tidied that to death too. It was starting to happen in the Dordogne. This church was the official RAF church where pilots came to pray before missions, but the Holy Ghost would feel out of place among all these rolls of honour. Tom lit a candle to liven things up. The thought of going to Patsy's flat after work cheered him. But perhaps after all he should go home to be with Beth. Take her to the movies or something. They could see the new Bertolucci.

Paul was following Tom now, his face sallow in the half-light.

'Marry her then,' shouted Tom, suddenly inspired. 'Marry her if that's what you really want. Disraeli's wife was years older than him. And so was Raymond Chandler's, twenty years, if I'm not mistaken. Nobody loves you like your mummy.' He bent down and peered at a golden casket, watching Paul's reflection, studying his hesitation. 'Good Lord, frankincense and myrrh in a golden casket.' The battle for Beth invigorated him; he couldn't stop talking. 'Don't muck about. Put your life where your heart is.' Phrases of that kind spilled from his lips. He had the better of Paul. He was waltzing. 'Tomorrow I'll see about a divorce, a quickie.'

'What the hell's got into you? You're a bit . . . precipitate, aren't you?'

'Beth hasn't time to waste, old sport. So none of this

22

*mañana* stuff. None of this let's do it in some dim distant future that never arrives and then off you skedaddle at the first grey hair. Now or never, that's your choice – and speaking as the responsible first husband I have to insist that you accept this ultimatum.' He put a bear-like arm around Paul and lowered his voice. 'But if you don't feel you can go ahead with it . . . the kindest thing, the only thing to do is to nip it in the bud, disappear before too much harm gets done. You know. Women.'

Paul dislodged himself. 'Have you gone crazy? Don't you think Beth should have a say in all this?' He raised one sardonic eyebrow and Tom panicked.

'Oh, I've talked it over with her. No secrets between us. Never have been. She absolutely doesn't want to go on like this. Been crying all night. She'd rather you commit yourself or sod off.'

'That is the ultimatum cooked up by the two of you in your cosy, sexless, nuptial bed?' Paul's voice was at its coldest, its most fastidious.

'Absolutely,' lied Tom, refusing to be goaded.

'But you appeared quite shocked when I mentioned marriage a few minutes ago . . . '

'Not shocked, dear boy, not shocked; just frightened, for the two of you.'

'Frightened?'

'Well, you know . . . the age gap; the ticking clock . . . '

Tom was not habitually a liar. In fact he had a reputation for honesty, but there were times when one's back was against the wall, when lies saved the day. God, one cliché after another. Good thing he didn't write the way he thought. He'd have to fire himself.

Tom repeated his lie again and again, embroidering a bit more every time, as the two men padded up and down the aisle.

At last Paul spoke, squeezing out the words. 'I'll need a bit of time.'

He was just a child, thought Tom, posing elegantly as a man. 'Take the weekend. But let me know. Let me know on Monday morning. No point in prolonging the agony.'

# FOUR

A fly circled the ceiling. It must have been hiding in
the folds of the curtain. Nothing else seemed to be
happening. But everything was happening. He could hear
his stomach gurgle. If he lifted up his hands they were a
stranger's. A decision had to be made. This hand could be
covered in blood.

'Christ!' He sat bolt upright, sprang out of bed, peed;
shook away the drips, put on a Brandenburg, did his
press-ups, made coffee, ignored the telephone. He had
at least made one decision already: he would under no
circumstances answer the telephone. It could be his mother.
It could be a friend. It could be her.

The phone went on and on. He took the coffee to the
window-seat and stared out at Markham Square. Two girls
in studded black leather mini-skirts walked by, but he knew
they'd revert to type in a few years: tweeds and horses and
headscarves and holding the family fort. He sighed and
turned back and looked coldly at his small hygienic flat
(except the rogue fly). Those girls probably expected to
marry someone like him and die happily ever after. On
paper he was eligible.

The coffee went cold, undrunk. Making decisions is hard
to do with the frontal lobes; that was a known fact. But he

didn't have the leisure to let the decision make itself; let his solar plexus work it out and all that stuff. Really he should just know what to do instinctively, the way (he presumed) most mothers knew they couldn't give up their child, no matter how poor they were, how hopeless their prospects. God would provide, or not.

He got dressed and went down to the Thames. At Battersea Bridge he walked along the embankment and leaned over the wall looking at the houseboats. Pop tunes drifted out from one barge called *The Merry Purr*. Young folks having fun; no responsibilities yet. Beth's cat hadn't had a merry purr, not once, not even when he joined her in her big nuptial bed in the afternoons. It had been a bloody nuisance. And stank the house out. It was the only thing that he didn't like about Beth, that she could tolerate that vile smell. A young couple emerged from *The Merry Purr*. They seemed to be quarrelling. They walked over the planks while he lectured her on fickleness. The boy looked like a tormented poet, poor sod. The girl was all vitality – there was something odd about her though, as if she was pulled in opposite directions by enormous pressures and would soon burst into fragments. Oh well, they would either stay together or – more likely – not; and meet in future decades across crowded rooms, nodding politely. Entropy was the law; sooner or later; *why not sooner?* Save the whole heartbreak of it, the struggle to hold on to happiness, like a fistful of water.

The sun was very red and very low in a grey, ungiving sky. The river sluggish and the tide low. A dingy swan stabbed its beak at a floating plank. Around the corner was Westminster: the centre of the universe. If earth had not anything to show more fair then it was in a bad way.

Paul pushed up his collar and walked on towards Pimlico, keeping on the riverside all the way. Why was it that one felt that by looking at huge expanses of water one would be able to gain perspective on one's life? A rose hue through the clouds hinted at a particular Turner in the Tate. Dusk came, grimly punctual, like bills. A colder wind began to whip his ears. He should have worn his Russian hat, the one he bought in Leningrad, training with No. 2. A top-floor window opened in a block of flats and a pair of anonymous hands threw reams of torn-up paper into the sky. Scraps of white specks floated down, a flock of doves, eddying on the breeze; some whirled to a stop at his feet. He picked up a piece and read '*ove*'. Had it been '*Love*' or had it been '*over*'? Someone jealous, perhaps. Someone disillusioned. Someone clearing their desk. Clearing their life. It was always satisfactory clearing out one's life; throwing away old boxes of clobber, old clothes, old habits, old threats.

He tried an experiment; tried to imagine that some other perfectly wise and sane soul inhabited his predicament, his being; a soul that did not run on his own neurotic grooves; for how could he not, to some extent, be neurotic: a twentieth-century white, educated, spoiled, male? What would that perfectly sane soul decide in his situation? What would he do if he loved and was loved by a perfect woman: fifteen years older than himself?

He scanned the Thames and frowned. Presumably loving a great treat of a woman like Beth was a reaction to his obsessional mother, who doled out bits of herself like cheese in wartime. How trite. Love had to be more than a reflex. He walked into a tobacconist and bought himself a pipe and tobacco. These props might help him. They seemed to go with the sane idea.

Stuffing the pipe gave him confidence. He would know exactly what to do by the time he had smoked it. But the wind blew the smoke back into his eyes. He should never have tampered with journalism; never got into that louche, seductive world in the first place. Doll Tearsheet; Beth Scrutton.

After a while he climbed the steps of the National Gallery, handing in his coat and umbrella, and made for the Renaissance. It had always reinforced him in moments of stress at Oxford, particularly *St Nicholas Rebuking the Tempest* by Bicci di Lorenzo. The saint on deck wagging his finger reprovingly at the storm clouds, oblivious of the sea nymph, naked and alluring, swimming near the rudder. How sad for the saint not to know the nymph was below, not to be able to pull her up gently from the depths, wet and glistening and grateful. But perhaps the saint was wise, and one should stay in one's own element.

Today he sought out a favourite Piero della Francesca, and for the first time noticed that St Michael appeared to have severed his own foot in the process of cutting off the dragon's head.

'I can't stand all the chocolate-box madonnas,' said a young man walking by him, determined to hold himself back from the suction of dead genius. The girl who trailed after had that air of someone trying too hard to please. She muttered something uncontentious, but Paul could tell that the madonnas attracted her no less than their divine offspring, whose etiolated or chubby fingers pumped at a series of holy breasts. She would inevitably marry the conceited young man and bear his children and turn a blind eye to his indifference until happiness with the opposite sex would seem like some unnatural and dangerous fantasy which could only create discontent. But, on paper, they were eligible. The girl 25, the man about 30. How convenient.

Motherhood was behind Beth. She had been a madonna twice. He wished he had known her then. Yes. He wished she was young. Once he had admitted that to himself he felt a great sense of release. He stood in front of St Michael for another minute, looking at his implacable face. You could see he meant business. Pity about the foot.

## Beth 1969

On leaving the gallery he sensed that a decision had started to coalesce. The sensible one. Bound to hurt both parties. But in the long run, *wise*. He walked back to his flat briskly, stopping off to buy frozen Chicken Kiev for supper. He opened a bottle of Chardonnay and sat in his room in the lamplight listening to Mozart on Radio Three. The phone rang. But he didn't answer.

When he woke on Sunday morning he lay despoiled by his dream. He had hauled Beth up from the deep waters, rescuing her from the cutting edge of a rudder. She slid into his arms, wet, glistening, smooth, ineffably smooth, like the beautiful serpent slaughtered by St Michael. It was a wet dream in every sense, and he woke in pleasure, but then when he opened his eyes to the stark day his stomach ached with anxiety. The pendulum-swing of decision-making shuddered back and forth in his gut.

After drinking two cups of coffee and sitting for ages on the lavatory reading the *New York Review of Books* he put a cushion on the phone, but he could still hear its muffled cries. Then he put three cushions on it and felt he was smothering an unwanted baby. Beth wouldn't be able to have babies any more. *She was too old.* Maybe she'd stop her periods soon; become menopausal; shrivel up or shine with whipped-up energy. Her hair would go grey and wiry. Grey. Her stomach would bulge. Her lips would show signs of mortality. He would be 47, in his prime, powerful, solvent, in mid-flight; she would be 64, an old woman in black.

He shaved very close that morning and took special care with his nails. Even he approved of his hands; hands couldn't be too good-looking. Somewhere he had always known that ecstasy was as slippery as an eel; it was not of this world; the gods were jealous; they always contrived something to spoil things, always cracked the jar, took a chip off the porcelain.

Perfection, ecstasy, rapture was a dream. Those who live for bliss live sterile lives. And how enviable to have the poise of those without passion. Licentiousness was all right. It stayed in its particular area of operation; did not swamp the world. But still it would be nice to be able, just once, to rescue one fantasy from the fire, carrying it wrapped in a blanket (singed but singing) to refute the wise old pessimists, the bill-payers and clock-winders. He would do the right thing.

At dusk he sat on a bench on Hampstead Heath watching an uncanny sun disappear. Birds landed with a skid on still water, their webbed feet descended and opened in the nick of time.

Down on the lower slope he had once sat with Beth. It seemed like the olden days but it was only a few weeks ago. It was the only time they ever walked on the Heath. She had told him a funny story about when she was young, reading on the Heath, resting on a blanket, immersed in her book. She forgot the time, having set an old Woolworth's alarm clock to remind her when it was getting late.

Suddenly two things happened at once. She saw a man flashing at her and the alarm jangled with terrifying loudness. The man jumped, scampering away like a hare, clutching his flies.

Paul smiled, tears falling down his cheeks and into his mouth. He couldn't stop them, but it didn't matter because he was sitting alone in the rain. And they never got to spend that night in Dieppe. At my funeral, he thought, the wrong people will be the noisiest grievers.

He jerked up suddenly. What the hell was he doing? It was crazy, destructive; puritanical death. Just because of some ultimatum probably concocted by a fickle husband, perversely possessive as they always are. But the grim fact still remained, beating away in his brain: Tom had told him that the idea of an ultimatum was Beth's. Not his.

He had said so, walking up and down the church, told him how he and Beth had talked it through and through and inside out and upside down and agreed in the end that it must be all or nothing. The honeymoon was over. Marriage or quit. Tom and Beth were each other's Best Friends. (Both of them at some time or another had used that phrase: *we are best friends.*) A united front against the world (including marauding lovers). Beth didn't want or warrant mere dalliance; to be ditched when old and grey . . . when the pain would be far more terrible than now, after just a few weeks of fun and when – how had Tom phrased it? – 'there's still a spring in her step' (yes, spring and summer in her step). It would mean heartbreak; that banal thing, the worst thing. Had he ever known it really? Maybe, tritely enough, at boarding school. He knew it's not just the heart that breaks but an inner spring; leaves one too cautious; comfortable with compromise, dreariness; preferring to go into battle than into love.

His pendulum thoughts swung back and forth as he sat there, getting soaked. He should leap at once into a taxi and rush over to her place now. She would be in that room, so alluringly shambolic, telling herself the endless death-adder hiss of his telephone was caused by some technical fault; not by a deliberately removed receiver; telling herself not to leap into a taxi likewise and come to him. He stood up and shook off the rain and the prospect of endless tears. Please God she wouldn't do that; wouldn't turn up and face him before he delivered the death blow; before he fled. He couldn't bear to see the mess she would be. He couldn't bear to see her plead. Would she plead or would she be proud? He would never know. He couldn't bear to see the butcher hack the beast in half, although he was a carnivore.

To avoid a scene he stayed out until two in the morning, sitting in the Everyman Cinema watching *Pandora's Box* for the umpteenth time until he knew every shot, every grain of shadow on Louise Brooks's irresistible young face; until each movement of each bit-player (all in German-expressionist turmoil) was part of his own pessimism and self-disgust.

Early on Monday Paul went straight into Tom's office and told him of his decision. Tom agreed to break Paul's contract and offered him the Washington column on a permanent basis. He could write it from London. He would not send Chewed Rope there after all, but put him on the Sports Page.

Paul refused all offers and said he was going to apply to the Foreign Office for a transfer somewhere in Europe. Meanwhile he went down to Sussex to stay with his mother.

Tom came home with a funny look on his face. But Beth didn't see it, bent over the bath as she was, washing her hair (in case). She heard the door slam and called down, through the gush of water, 'Gosh, you're early.'

He moved heavily into the living room and began to build up the fire. But something in him was satisfied, as if he had restored a garden wall; done a nasty but necessary job. He was not just the office Georgie-Porgie pudding and pie and crumpet; he took marriage seriously; his marriage.

Mostly he was a consciously moral man. Strange how easy and natural it had been to lie to Paul; going on and on about how Beth was totally in agreement with the idea of an ultimatum; making out it was her idea; like that time he needed the spare part for a lamp and, finding it impossible to get, had stolen it from a similar lamp at John Lewis's. He had done it swiftly and with an almost professional alacrity which had surprised his honourable, normal self.

Beth padded into the room, smiling, a pink towel wrapped around her shampooed hair, a little bit of foam still on her temple, a dressing gown tied loosely. But there was anxiety in her eyes. Strange how dear she was to him; yet so unsexy, even now; even now when he'd killed for her.

He glanced away and busied himself unnecessarily with the fire, returned to the sofa and patted the maroon cushion next to him with an odd abruptness. She lifted up a packet of cigarettes with stiff fingers. 'It's Paul, isn't it. Out with it.'

'He's moving on, old love. Leaving us. Getting posted abroad. Our man in Havana . . .'

'Leaving,' she said, stupid with fear; the darkness beginning.

He stared at the fire; he couldn't drag his eyes away from it. She heard him speak when the dizziness in her head allowed her to. He was saying something about some sort of ultimatum; being dumped when old and past it; responsibility of a husband; his love for her; his serious talk with Paul; his are-your-intentions-honourable routine, as if he were her old miner father all over again poking the coal fire and saying to Tom all those years ago, 'Marry her or bugger off, boyo . . .'

Once again the men were deciding her fate between them. She stared venomously at her husband's back. He was saying, 'Didn't want my baby made a fool of in a few years' time now, did I?' He was waiting to be congratulated.

'But I would have had those years, you fool.' She spoke in such an unfamiliar voice he turned round to stare at her.

He saw a woman with a bloated face, inflamed, as if it would burst open. He tried to light the cigarette she was clutching, but she flinched violently.

'You interfering shit. After all your escapades you dare to . . .' She was panting. Her eyes reddening with broken blood vessels.

Tom turned back to face the lesser heat in the grate and said in a sullen voice, 'He was going to string you along and then scarper . . . vamoose. You could have had a breakdown, you know. Think what effect that would have on the children. They still need us to be strong, like rocks. You were in it over your head.'

Over her head. And the more she struggled the more she would sink. She looked at her husband's back, that rock upon which she had built her rock-like house. She sprang upon him, scratching and clawing and biting, her gown flying open to reveal swaying breasts.

Tom lashed out with one violent sweep of his arm, thinking it was the mad cat attacking him and that this time he would pulverize it. His wife fell with a thump, legs splayed, ugly now; no, more than ugly, hideous.

He saw what he'd done and tried to lift her in his arms, but she shook him off. He stood back, wiping his face, while she slowly got to her feet and hobbled over to the window, pressing her head against the pane. Outside it was dark, dark and pitiless. Two men had betrayed her. Her lover and that other uxorious bond: years of loyalty, skivvying, baby-rearing, loving service, all down the sewer. She would never forgive Tom. Her Best Friend! *Hah.* As for Paul, that *coward.* Yes, she had never faced it before – he had a weak, feline streak. He wouldn't fight for her. She took one deep breath. She must fight for her own life. Perhaps this crisis was the crisis that would change things for the better. Tom being possessive, deceitful, dog-in-the-manger, clinging on to Mummy. She must fight. She would hail a taxi now, go over, break Paul's windows and false scruples, reason with him. She didn't give a fuck about happy-ever-after, gold wedding bands and stuff; she wanted what had so magnificently begun to run its course: to experience this love, this rapture, this fulfilment. NOW. All her life she had been played like a piano, with bits of broken tunes;

now all the scales were striking in harmony – so why did it have to stop before the end?

Yet somewhere she knew the damage was done; like the beast who stands alert after the *coup de grâce*, just for a moment; knowledge of its own death in its eyes.

The street sweeper saw the woman in the house that gave the best tips at Christmas. She was weeping at the window. Her face all blurred, squashed against the glass. Then she continued to bang her head against the glass. But it didn't break. The glass didn't break.

# TESS

## *1974*

*Foreigners belong in France because they have always been here and did what they had to do there and remained foreigners there. Foreigners should be foreigners and it is nice that foreigners are foreigners and that they inevitably are in Paris and in France.*

Gertrude Stein, *Paris France*

# FIVE

Tess Deutch sat in a bar in a nondescript corner of Paris watching the view. With so many trees in the city you could see spring approach, but the heavy rain pushed it back. She felt happiness rise in her like the steam from the faulty coffee machine that shrouded the café in mist.

A schoolboy ran along on the opposite side of the street holding his jacket over his head, turning to stare through the glowing window of the *boulangerie* where the stacked *pâtisseries* shone. She pressed the cup to her chin and watched a dog, tied up to a spindly tree, strain to get under the awning. An old woman came out of the *boulangerie* with a *pâtisserie* box tied in elaborate frills. In a single arabesque she put up her umbrella and released the dog without dropping the box.

The wall by the steps leading down to the Vietnamese section was ancient and pitted with bullet holes; rain gathered in them then suddenly gushed out again. A wizened Asian walked around puddles while the rain burst unregarded on his hairless head. Behind her the French barman polished glasses. Polished without looking at them. He could do it blindfold.

She put her cup down. She was free. Free of her mother. Free of old Vienna, free of romance, stale perfume, satin shoes slightly stained by champagne.

Last night in her hotel she had received another melodramatic phone call (she had to run down six flights in her nightie to the phone). It was one of her mother's usual rigmaroles. Sometimes she half wished her mother was extinct. She would turn her wishes into paper darts and send them speeding off down to the French coast, across the Channel, up past Croydon into London then up to Hampstead, straight through the letterbox into her mother's over-heated heart.

She would like to bundle her mother into a de-obsession box. It would look like Dr Who's police box, but instead of taking Mother through time and space to other planets it would shake her about till her teeth rattled and her obsessions with men flew out of her like demons from sanctified lunatics.

When Tess was a schoolgirl (a swot in a grey cardigan) she had sat in hotel rooms all over Europe writing letters to condemned lovers at her mother's husky dictation. This is how she spent her holidays. She would sit, hunched over a hotel desk, frowning, her tongue pressing at her tight orthodontist band, and copy endless letters ending endless affairs, e.g.: '*Dear Raoul. It was heaven, that night, that holiday in Venice, but, my love, I must be free, free*' – 'Underline the second free, my *Liebling*.' '*I'll always love you for swooping down on me like a giant . . .* ' – 'What's that bird, darling, the one that swoops suddenly?' '*Condor*.' 'Ah yes. You're getting very good at this, Tatiana – all right, all right, *Tess*.'

Outside the window of the café a man walked by, his arm around his girl. His hair was untidy but he had a witty smile. He stared into Tess's eyes and gave her the witty smile and she felt the beginning of some sad avalanche. When he continued on his way, his arm still around his girl, her sadness stayed with her. Then she pursed her lips and picked up her knitting. She was not going to get like her ridiculous mother, a reflexive romantic; reflexive and wrong, like those ducklings who follow a painted red beak.

In the corner by the pinball machine men of indeterminate age were huddled together talking in low voices. They showed no curiosity about the young woman near the window; she was nubile but she lacked style. Besides, she showed no curiosity about them. The rain kept sliding down the spindly tree, washing it clean of dog piss and fading even further the faded posters from the autumn of 1968: 'LA LUTTE CONTINUE'.

She sat there knitting for hours in a nondescript corner of Paris where the struggle continued, her face smooth and preoccupied. She finished a sleeve and was casting off when she looked up and saw the last stages of a French dinner party in the flat above the *boulangerie*. A stiff French dinner party. An old woman in maid's uniform was bringing forth the cheese, concentrating on the sacred board as befits a national monument.

At night the café had a different atmosphere; no melancholy charm, no barman dreamily polishing glasses. The evening staff had been specially selected for venom. How else could they control the *maquereaux* and *putains* of the night?

A Yugoslav looked at her. He had come from Dubrovnik with no assets but his heroic looks. Tess was thrilled, despite herself.

The movement around her was gathering the force of the snakepit. She ordered a Pernod, for its colour. Anything rather than go back to her hotel room on the sixth floor, next to the man who coughed.

A short, fat girl with bold eyes and the resilient look of a bounce-back doll said, 'Never seen you here so late, Miss Knitter. My name's Stella.' She sat down heavily, her legs well apart to ease the pressure and rub of each thigh. It was a good vantage point, by the door.

It turned out that Stella was not a tart, but she had her rules.

'They've got to be handsome. A man yesterday. Disgustingly fat, but he stuck like glue. Had to go to the Ladies to escape him. But when I peeped out he was still there. So I told him I was married with five children. Won't have them fat.' She reached plump fingers into Tess's glass, extracted the ice-cube and sucked at it like a starved Biafran. 'I saw this *dish*. Skinny. Dark. Nice dark stubble, like, you remember that movie star – Montgomery Clift? We went home and while he was on top of me I got so bored I ate a cream cake.'

Tess giggled and put away her knitting. Knitting for company had its limits.

'Looks don't always guarantee performance, do they, chickadee?'

Stella came from the Bronx and couldn't stand to be alone. 'No use staring at him. He's booked solid. Has to service an old French lady who buys him all that jewellery.'

That scotched Tess's interest in the Yugoslav.

'Have you got a shower in your hotel, for emergencies? Sometimes, late at night, you know . . . '

'I could smuggle you in when the patron isn't around. But it's down the hall. You have to pay.'

Two identical twins came into the café, walking stiffly as if carrying books on their heads. They moved in unison. They picked up their drinks in unison. They dressed exactly the same: dark polo-neck jumpers and dark trousers. They were the same height and their beards were the same length.

'They're not twins, honey. They're lovers. It's the old, old story of Narcissus. I guess if one has a bit of spinach on his teeth, the other puts a bit on his; and then they both dash it away simultaneously.'

Stella got stuck into white wine. Mae West without the satin and fur, but with that same cynical zest. She didn't so much seize the day as get it into a half-nelson.

'Oh God, look who's here.'

42

An American came over who was a familiar figure in every Paris bar. He flicked open his address book, which was as large as a telephone directory, and made a note of Tess's name and present address. He also made a note of her horoscope and asked her if she would like to come to his apartment to be photographed in the nude. But he soon became more interested in Francine, who had just wafted over to their corner.

But the girl-collector was out of luck tonight. When Francine cruised the bars it was not for a roll in the hay. She was a romance-junkie, and how she suffered in public! She pulled at cigarettes like a lamb on a dead teat. No matter how much smoke and coffee she imbibed, or lovers, she could never be assuaged. There was an emotional tapeworm inside her that gobbled up everything too fast.

'Do you like this green eyeshade?' she demanded of everyone. 'What's your name? Tess? So very English. Oh, you were christened Tatiana. Was your mother Russian? Not really? Now what's that supposed to mean?' Francine always spoke English to ex-pats. Listening to their French was like watching someone take a knife to the surface of an inlaid mother-of-pearl cabinet.

As the night wore on others joined them, including the Yugoslav, who complained about his workload, emitting roars meant to convey jocularity but reminding Tess of a penned-in and wounded beast. He should be striding the hills above Dubrovnik, his eyes reflecting the Adriatic. But he had walked out on all that to become a gigolo.

Students from the Sorbonne in Mao-ist jackets filed past their table full of idealism and contempt. Stella hurried off in pursuit of a hapless tourist, and soon afterwards, as Tess was sticking her needles into the ball of wool, preparing to go, she saw the man she thought of as 'my Englishman'.

It was Paul Radcliffe she was looking at. Paul married off

now. Father of a baby girl. A successful, still young diplomat doing his Paris stint. He never dabbled in journalism these days. All that riff-raff. But sometimes he and his wife liked to escape the formality and protocol of the Embassy and slum a bit in cafés like this.

Tess had seen him (her secret heart-throb, her mother would have said) only once before. It had been in this café with the same rather wistful woman. That time he had stared at her with concentration as if recruiting her for something. And his face had kept her awake that night.

She had read somewhere that foot soldiers used to scour the land to find delicacies to feed captured princes, believing them to be unable to survive on their own rough fodder. They would have scoured the whole kingdom for this man.

But there was something wrong with him all the same. He seemed to be sulking; turned away from the woman, who was leaning towards him on the spindly chair, face slightly averted as if from a rebuke, her skin drawn tight on her narrow, irregular features.

The other night his eyes had sparkled when he stared at Tess. She was a distant field. She looked greener. She had turned away firmly. But his face stayed with her as if its image had been waiting in her mind like an undeveloped negative for the right components to bring it to light. His eyes were humorous. Among all the professional Valentino eyes in the bar they were humorous, and ironic.

Tonight the couple sat in silence. They could have been strangers in a lift. Tess willed him to look up at her again. She wouldn't look away nervously this time. She had been rehearsing how not to; preparing herself for it. She always looked away, walked away, even ran away from anyone who tried to pick her up, as she would take her hand from a hot stove.

But he didn't notice. Didn't perceive her thought rays. So

much for fatal attraction. What was he doing in a low joint like this anyway? Slumming? Or just doing what she was doing, watching the ex-pats and the natives?

But later, while she is discussing the meaning of fate with her new fateless friends, Paul does notice her again, the dowdy English girl with the knitting. He notices her old eyes. In her eyes he sees a sad knowledge of practicalities, a circumspection, an ability to keep secrets, deliver documents by night, pour poison into chalices with the demureness necessary for the job. Or perhaps he sees none of this, only a nice sensible English girl who would make a good nanny for their baby, Grizelda. They didn't trust the girl they'd hired from the agency.

The rue Mouffetard was a seething market on sunny mornings and not yet given over entirely to North Africans and their sticky cakes. A man had a bear on a rope, a sight from the Middle Ages no one else seemed to be marvelling at. Another stood with a shawl of unskinned rabbits round his body. Tomatoes and apricots poured out of sacks on to fast-emptying stalls. Tess picked up a French tomato. It shone from within. How different from the wan inhabitors of cling-film in London shops. Bred in Holland under artificial light, tasting of Dutch rain. (But, despite her francophilia, she knew somewhere in the home counties, far away, fat and jolly Falstaffian tomatoes flourished in good summers.)

A flower-barrow gave her an idea for a jumper. She had confided in one of the Beaux Arts students last night that she would like to put water-lilies like Monet's on the jumpers she knitted, and he had given her an angry lecture on sentimentality, insisting that for Monet to paint water-lilies while human beings suffered was escapist crap. Tess had hung her head, but today innocent joy gave her confidence in her ideas.

She cruised down the market and, while she was dithering over cheeses, she saw that Englishman again. Had he been following her?

'You were at the café last night,' she remarked brightly, 'with a young woman with short dark hair.'

'My wife, Alison.'

She felt a routine disappointment. 'I can't make up my mind between the Pyrénées or the Cantal.'

'Why not take both?'

'A very masculine solution.'

'Ah, you think one should be monogamous with cheeses?'

'Are you over here on holiday?'

He told her his name was Paul Radcliffe. He was married, so she was not going to pay much attention. He even referred to a baby named Grizelda. He was doubly unavailable. He had no right to be so attractive. To be close to such gorgeous men is painful, when one is aged 18, especially when one has only casual acquaintances for company; the larky talk of drifters and barflies – snatching at the hem of the night. But even his black coat exuded a power that caused her voice to soften, slow down, deepen; her pupils to dilate under the awnings, her hands to tremble a little as they touched the *chèvres* to see how ripe they were, loving the way the straw stuck to them, straw all the way up from the Auvergne.

Resolutely insouciant she turned away from Paul and waved goodbye. He said, 'You must come and have a drink. We live near the Luxembourg Gardens in a rented flat in a Count's mansion, opposite the Deaf and Dumb Institute for Children. We're lucky. Right in the middle of Paris and we have a country view – of their huge garden.'

He poured charm. Charm and reserve combined. A perfect balance for an English diplomat with a great future ahead of him. A trifle conceited perhaps. Few women would have the confidence to vie for him. She knew that if she tried she'd spill her coffee, fake her reactions. But in some shrewd layer of her being that had been born old, she did wonder if inside that resplendent figure there could be a thwarted little boy.

# SIX

Paul has done the sensible thing. Why is he then so unhappy? Why does he take it out on his wife in those long, shrapnel silences, his disinclination to reach for her in the night?

He has noticed the skin drawing tighter and tighter on her face; her eyes shifting anxiously; the baby cries all the time as if she's teething, but she's not yet teething.

He looks out over the garden wall where two deaf and dumb children play with a ball, their curious cries like the cries of some unknown Amazonian water-bird, rending the dusk. In the corner hotel the lights are already blazing, and in a high room the blind is undrawn and a naked couple embrace, exhilarated by the eyes of neighbours upon them. They unclasp for a moment and wave to him. He looks down at his child. She has such an obdurate head. That tender, throbbing place in the centre is slowly closing up. How odd of evolution to labour for millions of years and come up with infants with open craniums at birth. So appallingly vulnerable. How do so many people survive, apparently intact, when they all require so much delicate handling, so much protection? The fontanel, the fontanel. The word swings in his mind like a bell.

They were going to an Embassy 'do'. The social treadmill that was part of the job.

He had arranged for the English girl, Tess, to babysit again. She needed the money and she was very good with Grizelda. She had the touch. He'd known she would. He was seldom wrong about character. And mercifully she held no sexual attraction. Any minute now she would turn up with her knitting and he and Alison would be free.

'Do you like my new Laura Ashley?' His wife stood at the door, dressed with too much flowery grandeur for the occasion. The other diplomats' wives would be in tailored clothes; discreet colours.

She was standing so awkwardly there at the door, her nose red and shiny, a strange conglomeration of curls pressed high on her head, making her look chinless.

'It's a bit much. Haven't you got anything more . . . *subtle?* No, I suppose you haven't.' His voice had turned nasty again. She jumped as if stung, her cheeks wobbling, and retreated. He turned back to the orgy at the window; the trouble with being a saint, trying to be at least, was that it was hard to sustain. You could make sacrifices; relinquish joy; then you had to live with the consequences, the plod down the years; the curse of having done the 'right thing'. And the strain comes out in rudeness. He hated his wife for bringing out this rudeness in him. Good manners were for him, at least in theory, the first of the cardinal virtues, and he was abusing his personal ethic every day.

The drip of his badly disguised irritation was wearing her down. If you could judge a man by the health and gloss of his wife, he would be found wanting.

He picked up the baby-brush and began to brush Grizelda's hair: soft, gentle strokes that instantly stopped her whimpering. It worked like a magic charm. Brush, brush, brush; she gurgled, she curled up her toes; she gazed up at him as if his face were the crucible of all being. To hell with the cavorting couple in the window, to hell with the idiocies of sex; this was the only thing that mattered.

When Tess arrived to babysit, Alison looked pale and sombre in a grey suit, a little baggy at the seat, although it was comparatively new. Alison didn't seem to have a shrewd eye for tailoring. She handed Tess the squalling infant. 'It must be wind,' she said, as she always said, moving away to get 'Woodward's Celebrated Gripe Water' (she had it sent from England). As soon as she handed over the baby to Tess it stopped crying, as usual, which as usual was a bit embarrassing. But it was easy to see that Alison was too tense, and babies pick that up.

If this babysitting job led to more babysitting and that part-time job selling posters at the Galerie Maeght really came through, Tess could postpone her return to London, and to hell with the secretarial course, at least for a few months. Not only that, two women she'd met in a *tabac* one morning had offered to pay decent money if she knitted them an English pullover like the one she wore everywhere, with the phoenix pattern. They all loved phoenixes; firebirds; D.H. Lawrence symbols; *passion*. But the trouble with phoenixes is that they can't function without ash. Lots and lots of ash. How was she going to knit in the ash? She wasn't going to knit the bird without it as she had done so lazily for her own sweater. She wanted to perfect the design; maybe go professional. And she knew precisely what she wanted it to look like. It was just a matter of getting the pattern meticulously right.

After Mr and Mrs Radcliffe left the house Tess cuddled the baby for a while, stroking and rocking it. Every time she touched the side of the baby's cheek it would instantly turn to suck whatever had touched it there, moving star-like hands about vaguely in the air in a pumping motion as if somewhere there must be a maternal breast in the void. It was funny, babies were born with this reflex to suck and humans were born with the reflex to worship – therefore at some time or another over the misty centuries God must have existed, as solid and beneficent as a breast; it was only logical, wasn't it?

'Do you think Tess is going to be all right? She's only eighteen. We don't know her very well, yet we give her such responsibility,' said Alison querulously as Paul drove towards the rue St Honoré.

'Steady as a rock. You could go into the jungle with that one. The kind that couldn't live with herself if she didn't do the right thing. We've been lucky to find her. And she's so cheap.'

'Another illegal worker in Paris.'

'There's no reason she shouldn't get a work permit if she gets that job in the gallery. Then we'll be well set up. I don't like hiring agency people. I read about one who put the baby in the oven and . . . '

'Don't.' Alison blocked her ears. Ever since she'd given birth she couldn't bear to hear of any crime or atrocity. And the only films she could bear to see were gentle old-timers from the thirties or thereabouts, before people began to skin each other alive and gouge out each other's eyes in Technicolor. She'd even had to stop reading the paper because she began to cry at the first horror story: there was always someone tortured by the fires, by the flood, by famine, by war, or just plain tortured. Once, when she was breast-feeding, the *New York Herald Tribune* had become saturated with tears and oozing milk.

Being a mother, if it took, reduced you to one quivering nerve of empathy for all living things. You had to block your ears against the torrent of weeping and wailing. It came out of the newspapers, the television, the radio, people's eyes in the street; it came out of the ground; out of ancient history. The whole of humanity was roaring for a mother. All murderers were murderers because they were adopted, or put out to foster-parents; and you always knew they were going to be murderers because they began to torture kittens, put out the eyes of frogs with a needle; holding the squirming body firmly. Her brother had done that once. She hated him from then on and for ever. Did he remember the eye incident, or had he conveniently forgotten it, expunged it from his mind? It was on *her* mind. She thought she had forgotten it, but now it came back with greater ferocity to torment her.

As they drove past the rue des Ecoles she looked longingly at the cinema that specialized in old movies. This week they were showing Jean Gabin in *Le Quai des Brumes*. She longed to jump out of the car and go there now. She had a feeling she would like it. Go there and sit in the darkness watching an old *film noir*, so comforting in its romantic melancholy, its grainy charm; rather than have to endure another endless, brittle dinner party. She was invariably stuck at the end of the table with the other dull appendages.

Once – oh, the disgrace of it – she had sat at the table with tears coursing down her cheeks. She didn't know why. It was just the strain of all the small-talk. So exhausting, and when the hostess indicated that the evening was over, you could tell by the speed with which the guests fled how everyone had felt as she had done about this obscure duty connected with the Byzantine pecking order of the Embassy. But why had she cried like that? Nobody appeared to have noticed – or at least, they pretended they didn't, although tears splashed into her dessert of tropical fruit. Everything seemed tragic to her now, even a boring dinner party. Perhaps it was just her hormones bounding about her body out of control after their triumph of birth. Or maybe it was simply that her whole life with Paul – oh, she loved him so much; that she could ever have found such a man was incredible and against all expectations – but her life with him was *wrong* somehow. It was not just the Embassy functions that were brittle and nervy and false and hollow, but breakfast, dinner, lunch and tea as well; it was every waking hour with Paul. He seemed – she hesitated to form the thought – but he seemed, yes, barely to be able to tolerate her presence in his life. And yet it was he who had insisted on marriage. Absolutely insisted. Rushed her off her feet. As if the hounds of hell were after him. He had hinted of some *grand amour,* with an older woman. It sounded rather intriguing; she would have liked to have known more, so she could laugh it away, but he clammed up whenever she tried to draw him out. She gathered there had been a jealous husband making trouble of some kind. Sometimes she wondered, with misgiving, if she did not seem rather colourless in comparison with whoever she was. She even wondered if he had got the mystery woman totally out of his system and if, even though she was his wife and the mother of his child, she wasn't some pawn in their much grander game.

# SEVEN

'I've got a migraine, Paul. I can't go out tonight. My head's bursting.'

'Again?' Paul laid down his Schaeffer pen and turned wearily towards the familiar shadowy presence interrupting his concentration. Detestation was unpleasant when it took over the mind, because it also made one detest oneself. But then he had not taken himself seriously for a very long time; not since he failed his one great moral test. Having failed that, what was the point of all this? Love is not love that alters when it alteration finds. And that poor woman at the door. He was the culprit who had undermined her confidence. And the more he did it the more she clung to him like a limpet. The more she whimpered.

'Yes . . . and I'm afraid I can't get hold of Tess to put her off for tonight. She must be out somewhere with her pals and she's due here at six-thirty.'

It was raining that night; a monotonous drizzle that Paul quite liked. It was feeding the bulbs; it was dribbling right down to the roots of the horse-chestnuts. The prospect of a night without his wife was a relief. Not that she wasn't nice, intelligent, well-mannered etc. She was just the wrong person.

★   ★   ★

Tess was in yet another bar. In another mirror-lined room, its tiles decorated with thirties playboys in striped scarves, its waiters stern, their long white aprons without a stain; the cactus in brass urns. The ashtrays were the same green as the enticing doorways that led into courtyards. She opened them sometimes to glimpse shadows and cats and a sense of old stones, carved and worn pediments; even, sometimes, gargoyles placating the night.

The barman wove his tray through the crowd like a sailor on deck on a choppy night. The singer belted out *La Vie en Rose*. A gypsy tried her luck selling red roses to wooing Americans. Students from the Beaux Arts ate their way through the *plat du jour*. Everyone clapped at the end of the song and the singer, a battered charmer, prowled the room wearing a torn shawl, her nylons with crooked seams and her feet too old and fat for her high-heeled shoes. The Edith Piaf stereotype survived. And accordions were coming back on street corners because it was not only tourists but also the French who liked to hear them. The Americans went gooey about the little chained animals in dolls' beds at their feet.

'Ah, Dubrovnik . . .' The Yugoslav was crying again, huge tears that dropped unregarded on to his gorgeous rings. Tess had once organized a whip-round to raise money for his fare home, but when she gave it to him he pocketed it gratefully, embracing her, almost to death, and remained in Paris. He was having another one of his spectacular public glooms, his head in his hands, his fingers clawing his cheeks. Next he would flash the photograph of his peasant grandmother; murmur incoherently about his problems. She had stopped trying to draw him out and wondered if the photograph he kept pawing was of his mistress and not of the grandmother. Could he be a gerontophile? His face closed if she ever questioned him. They said he had once been in prison, presumably for theft or some irregularity in his papers. She grabbed hold of his wrist, which made him flame his eyes at her, and turned it over with deliberation. His gold watch revealed that it was time to babysit. She was always punctual. Sometimes she thought she was the only person in the world who was. Sometimes she thought the only thing Paul Radcliffe really noticed or admired about her was her punctuality.

She got the bus up Boulevard St Michel, but because of the rush hour she arrived late. Paul opened the door immediately, as if he had been on the other side stamping with impatience. He escorted her back down the stairs and out of the house, explaining that his wife had a migraine and would not be going out with him, so they did not need her services, but that he would very much like to buy her an aperitif before he shot off to the party.

Did she know that Zola had once lived over there? In a flat with a view of the Deaf and Dumb gardens? Cézanne used to visit Zola every week and dine on his mother's casserole. Perhaps he got the idea for Cubism standing at the window, digesting his casserole, contemplating the gardens, which were all laid out, as she must have observed, in squares, each with different densities of green, different heights of foliage.

They entered into the part of the Luxembourg Gardens called 'The English Garden', but despite romantic lawns and rustling shrubs it is not very English since it is littered with the statues of French cultural heroes.

Paul's umbrella was furled. He gripped its leather handle so tightly she could see the whites of his knuckles. The man was evidently under strain. He was only being polite, buying her this drink in Montparnasse, paying her off, keeping her sweet. But she couldn't be merciful and let him escape. Not yet. She would enjoy the few moments with him that fate provided.

Last night Stella maintained there was no such thing as fate. Fate was for the birds, like religion, something we invent to make us feel there is a meaning to existence. Then she had gobbled three éclairs in a row and puffed off to the bars for another gruelling night trawling the Left Bank. She was always so cheerful, Stella; meaninglessness made her merry, or perhaps she admired her own steely bravado in the face of such nihilism.

'Damn!' Paul's umbrella had got stuck. He couldn't open it and the rain was suddenly pouring down again. He stood there struggling with the wretched thing, at first with sweet reasonableness, then with increasing fury, until he tried to wrench it open by force. Spokes shot through stiff black fabric. He held it up for ridicule, water dripping down his eyelids. It was a botched job, a vulture run over by traffic, a bad omen.

There was a sentry-box round the corner in which they sheltered, peering out at the rapidly emptying gardens. They were silent, master and slave, suddenly thrown into embarrassing confinement.

'You should go home and dry off, Mr Radcliffe. Don't worry about me.' She thought he shuddered for a moment at the prospect. 'I can always put this over my head and run for it.' She held up her plastic bag of knitting.

He draped his coat over their heads, then led her through the black pines and dripping birches. Suddenly it was a black and white movie: the gardens an enchanted forest, a glade of winding paths without human footprint – veiled in the slanting silver rain. Over by distant tennis courts two lovers were strolling, faces held up to receive the rain. They were figures in a movie when movies were like that.

Envy gurgled inside her but she swallowed it. Paul had never, by so much as a raised eyebrow, a glance held too long, a purring of the voice, indicated any interest in her. He was just a decent chap in a foreign city desperate for a reliable babysitter who didn't get pregnant, have emotional scenes or steal Alison's perfume. He had to keep her sweet. He would buy her a drink now, then vanish away to his grand evening, and she would be left with her knitting and her inexhaustible street life.

Paul's arm was through hers and she was aware of the smell of his Floris soap and his manhood.

Rain thundered down on the merry-go-round, bounding off the waterproof cover of the rocking horses. They jumped puddles, scuttling out of the gate like a four-legged monster under the black cloak, keeping close to shop fronts. When they crossed rue Raspail the statue of Balzac loomed down on them; safe at last from his pestering creditors.

The waiter at Le Sélect recoiled from Paul's broken umbrella as if it were a dead cat. Paul led Tess through to a corner table and plonked down their sodden gear.

Rain always made her feel cosy, especially the sound of it on leaves. But there was that other sort of rain, rain falling from a dead sky. Rain that faded deck-chairs, rusted wrought-iron balconies, caused depression.

That was the sort of rain she thought of when Mother, deciding at last, at a vast age, to live with Gogol, used to say, 'Gogol – he brought me in out of the rain.'

'*Un Pernod, s'il vous plaît.*'

'Johnny Walker.' The waiter took their order and sidled off through the tables, now filling up as darkness deepened and rain showed no sign of easing up.

They watched the fire-eater of Montparnasse through the plate-glass window. His crowd was reduced to two Japanese dwarfed by umbrellas and a child with sopping parents. Behind them blazed the windows of La Coupole and a poster advertising a Charles Bronson movie. The French passion for Charles was a mystery.

It was too early to run into her gang. They usually moved up to trawl Montparnasse at a later hour, when flirtation took on a hunting edge. She was safe. Those two worlds should not collide. Paul wouldn't like them, too snobbish by half. It was some kind of frustration that was making him edgy in that English way, taking it out on his wife – and not so subtly either. Yes, she could see that; she was well aware of it and did not approve. Yet, oh, she wanted to be with him, *with him*.

'The waiter, isn't he wonderful, the *contempt*,' said Paul, then turned to watch the fire-eater on the pavement outside who performed with gusto, even though his audience had dwindled to a single child. He billowed out his cheeks like a frog; he paused melodramatically, then whooshed out dragon flames, making the boy jump in alarm.

'Fire in the rain,' Paul mused. 'Pretty.' For a moment she thought she saw boredom cross his face; was he wondering how he was going to slog through the next half-hour? 'Imagine them gargling petrol around in their mouths, setting it alight. You'd have to be very hungry to choose a métier like that.'

Even when the child was dragged away, the fire-eater kept it up, exhaling tongues of fire into the void. Paul said he must be making some kind of philosophical statement.

Tess drew out her tiny pack of cigarettes, Parisiennes, 20 centimes for four, in a French blue packet. She loved the blue colour, that was why she smoked them; just as she drank Pernod for its yellowy green. She was proud of the way she had made her earnings last without having to ring up Mother to ask for more. Mother had been thrilled by her decision to stay on and give the secretarial course in London a miss. Too thrilled. She probably had visions of her stalking around the bars, like Stella and Francine, but without their pathos.

'Some people never give up,' Paul said, finishing his drink.

She supposed he meant the fire-eater. How nice Paul looked with wet hair, as if he had been sweating. It made him less formal, less intimidating. To be in the Embassy he must be frightfully clever. In London he would never have met her. He was far too grand. Ex-pats always got thrown together, and there was no basis to it or substance. When they returned to their native lands everything evaporated; she knew that. She knew that although she was only 18. But then she felt like an old woman saddled with the body of a young girl. And that body burnt at inappropriate times for inappropriate people. 'It's lovely for us, of course, having met you, Tess. We had a series of awful babysitters, one so sinister we both insisted on returning home soon after leaving the house to get rid of her, because we had been so worried we were unable to eat, much less socialize; so your deciding to stay on in Paris has been a great boon to us. How did you square it with your parents?'

'Mother's the kind who understands everything to death. And I haven't got a father to speak of. Although there is a kind of unofficial one now, Gogol, but he came into my life a bit too late for it to be of much use.'

'Ah . . . ' He looked at her directly, a rare occurrence. 'Your mother is a hippie. She feeds you on pumpkin and lentils and allows you to come into the bedroom while she's in the throes of passion, and no doubt she christened you something far more romantic than Tess. Let's see . . . Mandala, River, Moonbeam, Sky . . . ?'

'Tatiana. You see, Mum's too old for hippiedom. The word is, I think, er, bohemian.'

'It amounts to the same thing, doesn't it?'

'No. Bohemians read books. Kick ideas around. And love affairs are approved of, but only if incredibly intense and involving suicide attempts.'

He laughed. 'What a scrupulous social historian you are.'

'It's an important difference. I'd have hated it if Mother had gone to bed with total strangers simply because it was fashionable.'

'It was a mysterious fashion. It passed me by, locked as I was in the Foreign Office.'

'Mother was too old for it. I was too young for it. But I think both of us would have refused, if invited to an orgy. Mother, because she was too interested in passion. Me, because I have a sense of the ridiculous.'

'Burdensome for you at times.' He accepted another of her cheap cigarettes although she'd never seen him smoke cigarettes before. He liked his pedantic little prude. He liked her voyeurism, her knitting as she watched the 'savage parade'.

'Was your mother a political animal?'

'First she was one thing. Then another. She could unzip herself out of communism or any kind of utopianism as soon as she heard good reasons why they wouldn't work. She was a . . . eureka-ist I suppose.'

'Very unlike so many of her friends, I bet. I bet they kept clutching their beliefs through Hungary, through Prague.'

'If they'd lost their beliefs, they'd have – disintegrated. Their dogmas were their sanity; they believed *despite* the evidence.'

How she adored him. He resembled a movie star through the veil of smoke. How long could it have been since he sat like this in a bar with a girl; without his wife; not being irritated? Beside them a couple kissed, one watching his own reflection all the time, the other, her eyes swooningly closed, lost in the kiss. By the bar Tess saw a man who, from the back, could have been the Yugoslav; only he could have such manly bearing.

'Look, there's someone there I think we should avoid. He'll weep about Dubrovnik. Show you photographs of his grandmother.'

'Let's get out of here.' Paul threw down the money, leaving a tip, and led her purposefully out of the café. He draped his coat around them once more, cloaking them in the darkness of mutual conspiracy, still holding his broken umbrella, feeling in the mood to play truant.

They scampered across the boulevard, taxis splashing puddles on their shins. The fire-eater exhaled flame at them. 'Not La Coupole,' she advised. 'Too noisy.' Besides, she'd be sure to meet Stella and Francine there, Stella with gimlet eyes, Francine with that irresolute look of unrequited something. She led him around the back to The Rosebud, which was almost empty. Desultory jazz played softly in the background. They chose a table under the mirror. She sat facing it, and look, there she was: young, pretty, eyes bright with future. I must remember this, she thought. *I must remember.* It was a game she had played all her short life; trying to trip up time, trying to strap it down in its headlong rush, leaving behind forced memories that stuck like burrs to a jumper. I'll remember this, she thought, milking the moment, perhaps just because she had a crush on Paul; or perhaps because she had been in so few rooms, up so few stairs, in so few interesting situations, she liked to relish each one. Soon she would let events roll out of her hands and disappear into the past; but not tonight, never tonight.

# EIGHT

The Rosebud was filling with *noctambules*, some of a sinister elegance. Why was it that slightly sadistic-looking men in beautifully made clothes were sexy? She was sure this was a disreputable observation. Something to do with controlled violence, but with the emphasis on controlled. Some of the night-birds were dud versions of Hemingway or Scott Fitzgerald. A war correspondent leaning against the mosaic pillar was reliving a raid over Vietnam, his combat noises hardly noticed in the din.

Paul's face was changing as they ploughed on through the hours. The stiffness had gone, the starched edges, and he seemed to have lost all track of time.

Like Scheherazade she began another story to postpone the evil hour, in this case of departure, not execution. 'Then Mum hired a carpenter. He was young, handsome, *doomed* the moment she met him. One day in some new flat somewhere, plying him with tea, gazing into his stupid eyes as he droned on about some clairvoyant who did wonderful horoscopes, who could always predict the future with accuracy, blah-blah-blah . . . my mother is always randy for the next thing, if you know what I mean . . . '

'Likes to peek up the skirts of the future.'

'Likes to skip the future – like you skip through a book –

for the plot. She was crazy about the future; wanted to fly into its arms.'

'While you're crazy about the past; always knitting the past together, it seems.' His laughter egged her on to further disloyalties.

'So she implored the young man to get his friend to do her horoscope and at once began to feverishly write down all the information he asked for, then suddenly realized – oh God – she'd have to give him the date of her birth. The exact year! And to this very delicious young carpenter chap, whom she'd had her eye on for a rainy day, and he would know her age!'

'*Quelle horreur.*'

'So she simply lied; dropped ten years.'

'She took the manly course, like Bertie Wooster.'

'She changed one teensy weensy little number, from 1923 to 1933. And had to pay forty whole pounds for a false horoscope!'

'She sounds terrific. What pride!'

'She says it's worth telling lies about that because even if the bitches and bastards can't find anything else to sneer at they can always sneer at your age.'

'Or be even meaner about lying about your age. It's a sort of verbal face-lift.'

He took off his tie and put it in his pocket. In her jocular way Tess was getting rather close to a nerve.

She stared at the hair curling through the crack at the top of his shirt. Her throat dried out, she began to cough.

Billie Holiday was singing 'I don't stand the ghost of a chance with you'. Embarrassingly appropriate.

'Another drink?' He stood up and went to the bar to chivvy along the waiter, now seriously overworked. He was away for the entire song and the beginning of Billie's next number, about how she'd gladly surrender to somebody, body and soul.

In the mirror she could see that she had changed completely. She was no longer the tight-lipped daughter of *une grande horizontale*. Not the prim, Victorian offshoot of a jolly Restoration duchess. She had climbed out from the maternal shadow. She was worthy of grand passion herself. Body and soul.

When he returned she stared at him indolently, feeling her eyelids go heavy as honey, waiting for him to make some lovely utterance to her and her alone. This was the way babies looked – huge, unprotected eyes like hers, her face porous, dissolving into the beloved one. This was the way Grizelda looked at Paul when he cuddled her. She'd always thought all that Freudian stuff about Oedipus and Electra wanting to screw their mums and dads was nuts, because how could a baby know the ins and outs of it? (She found it hard enough, and she was 18!) But now she understood. Freud simply meant that the baby wants to merge, join, become one with the parent, body and soul; and the only way to do that is dear old sex. But with eyes open, looking into Paul's eyes, which would be shining with love and spermatozoa. And that was why missionary style would always be best (face to face, heart to heart), the most profound, but only if it was with the desired one. She leant her head back and analysed the ceiling; how revelatory alcohol was!

Paul watched her; she was quite attractive. He hadn't realized it before, attractive and sympathetic and his for the taking. He wanted to take off his medals and armour; wanted to sit her on his knee and croon false drunken things; wanted to confide, weep a little, forget the Embassy, his mother, his wife and everything that ever required from him the decent, difficult, unhappy-making 'right thing'. He lusted after indiscretion, just a touch of it. He wanted also to speak her name, her name, her *name*.

When he began to speak it was with a strange, dragging slowness.

'Have you ever made a big mistake, Tess? A mistake that ruined your life?'

She was a touch disappointed, having prepared herself for a bit of romance. To get a break from the chiselled sadness of his face she looked around her. Girls eyed her sullenly; men watched her with a different look; maybe lowdown sex with a stranger would be a release.

'Mistakes? Millions of 'em. Not playing with the unpopular girl at one of my schools, so I still feel bad about it. I know it will tip the scales when I'm at the gates of heaven and I'll be sent down below. Letting a boy in a Rome hotel lock me in a cupboard; taking the wrong subjects at school . . .' She went on merrily. But suddenly – she was staring at the poster of Deauville at the moment she heard the 'click' that told her: *he wants to tell you something. Something about a mistake he made. Go back, you blithering idiot. Backtrack. Give him a chance to tell you. It will draw him closer.*

If she went on babbling, skipping along over the other side of the ravine that had just opened beneath her feet, under the pretence that no signal had been given, then she would never get another chance of intimacy with him. She stopped chattering, obeyed the bat-squeak in her head. Even his voice had sounded totally different when he asked her the strange question, as if it came from a different self, beneath the censoring brain.

Tess turned to look at him. 'Well, I'm too young to have ruined my life – give me time. Have *you* made a mistake like that, Paul?'

The sigh he sighed was deep. The pre-confessional sigh. His shoulders relaxed as he put down his yoke. He leaned back, his dark head squirming against the clouded mirror, shielding her from her own listening face.

'Oh yes. Yes. Yes. Yes. A very stupid mistake.' He closed his eyes. 'I've never been able to take myself seriously since.'

Fear fluttered inside her. Shouldn't he be confiding in someone else? Someone his own age? Someone he was at Oxford with? Someone at the Embassy? Not her. Take away this chalice he pressed to her lips. Secrets could be poison that penetrate the blood-stream; that you never get out of your system; because those with secrets have power.

And now Paul was able to do what he was aching to do: tell her about Beth. How he had betrayed Beth. How he had broken her heart and his.

# NINE

They talked until dawn, moving on to Le Dôme for breakfast, exhaustedly stirring sugar cubes into black coffees, shivering as if after a night of love. Indeed, the waiter was certain they were victims of a passionate *nuit blanche*. They had the same exhausted intimacy; the same spent look; *unravelled*, like her knitting in its squashed plastic bag.

She had just discovered to her dismay that somehow in the rigours of the long confession, maybe in the move from The Rosebud to Le Dôme at first light, her knitting had fallen off its needles.

'Croissants?'

'*Oui, s'il vous plaît.*'

Traffic was building up; the first lorries thundered along the boulevard and the eyes of Balzac looking down upon Montparnasse at the start of the new day were cratered with dangerous knowledge.

The indefatigable fire-eater had at last left his nocturnal beat. A dustman clothed in green jumped out of a van and hosed graffiti off Charles Bronson's moustache. The steel blinds rattled up; and over at the kiosk the newspaper seller began stacking *Libération*, *Figaro* and the *New York Herald Tribune*.

A man hurried into Le Dôme bearing a long wicker basket

stacked with baguettes and fresh croissants, from which the waiter selected two for them.

A group of tramps were huddled outside between shining puddles, lines of caked spume along their cracked, unkissable lips.

They swore among themselves; their eyes like clocks without hands. Would money save them? So much came down to money. Her mother was supported by Gogol now. Her mother had found refuge; but hadn't altogether settled down. Did she still have the old red cummerbund which at parties she used to produce with a flourish to wind around the hips of her present incumbent?

Tess never thought of her mother by her name, *Aurora*, because it was embarrassing and, she suspected, a total invention of her own, like so much else about her.

When the romance ended Mother never counted griefs and costs, never argued nastily about the ownership of records or books, and consequently travelled light. But the cummerbund, yes, she always insisted on the return of that. Tess wondered if Mother still had it and if she wound it, on special occasions, around the portly girth of Gogol. It must be a little shabby by now.

When Paul went to the *cabinet* Tess picked up stitches. How could you survive when you had lost the love of your life? Never having had the time to learn about their faults and failings, to give your heart balance; never having been worn down by the sight of them picking their teeth?

Beth was empowered by long absence to goddess status. She was probably just an ordinary, aging woman; a housewife in London, cleaning around the bathtub, worrying about flabby thighs. She probably had cellulitis.

When Paul returned, sprawling opposite her, shirt open at the top, sleeves rolled up, stubble distinct in the morning light, she began to knit furiously, clashing the needles together as if that could bring him to his senses. She knew what love goddesses were like. Hadn't she been her mother's secretary? One of the doves of Venus?

'And you?' Paul asked lightly. 'Have you ever been through the mill?' He was trying to get back on a different plane, of which he had about as much hope as rescuing a small canoe swept over the edge of Niagara Falls. She was so young; an inappropriate choice for his confidante. Perhaps. Tomorrow he might regret his outburst. But not quite yet. Not in the after-glow of release.

'Well, there was an Irishman once.' She glanced up from her needles with murky, remembering eyes. 'He led me on something wicked. Got me in flames. Much older. Married. He kept trying to push me into the changing rooms in department stores, or leap into the back of parked laundry vans, or steal into the bathroom of hotels at Paddington Station after taking tea in the lounge . . . ' She told her ridiculous *demi-vierge* story under the striped awnings that swayed in the morning breeze, fluttering shadows over the tablecloth and two haggard faces. 'When I became too intense he fled, of course. He didn't want *lerve*.' She showed her little flesh-wounds to the veteran.

He looked at her with his tired, sea-green eyes. 'I *hate* the sodding Irish.' He was angry on her account! What pleasure it gave her. In that instant the old pain vanished without a scar. Acknowledgement. That's what was needed in these matters of rejection. Acknowledgement of what one had been through. Otherwise resentment in its tiny laboratory starts to build, cell by invisible cell, its little cancers. She looked at him. He gleamed back at her, an escaped prisoner, his jowels heavy with bristle, his hand near hers. She put down her knitting. But before she could decide to touch his hand, be bold for once, risk rejection, the waiter arrived with their croissants, fresh and melting.

'So I left England immediately,' he said with his mouth full, 'after I made that decision not to marry Beth. Got posted to Warsaw where I met Alison. She was working for the British Council. Polish girls are lovely, of course, but there was something about Alison. Her Englishness. Her sense of irony, which I had been missing. We married.' He sighed and munched the croissant. 'I thought I'd forget the whole damn thing. Then we had Grizelda.'

God, she was tired. Suddenly. It hit her like the proverbial sledge-hammer. A *nuit blanche* would mean a *jour noir*. No dinner last night. Talk. Talk. Talk. And love unwrapped like a withered mummy to reveal the goddess perfectly refreshed within.

'I didn't understand myself at all, you see.'

She thought then of the huge abysses beneath the sea. To know oneself one would have to be an oceanographer of the heart.

They walked slowly across the dew of the Luxembourg Gardens, his black coat slung over his shoulders, still holding the broken umbrella. He had not been concentrating on the disposal of litter. She pointed to a convenient bin, but he held on to the brolly out of sheer fatigue, or some obscure stubbornness; having thrown away so much perhaps he adhered too tightly now to little things.

'Will you get into trouble at work? Not turning up last night?'

'To the party? No one will notice.'

It did not occur to her to ask him if he would get into trouble with his wife. Anyway, Alison was far too much of a doormat to make trouble.

Near the bust of Sainte-Beuve in his bed of yellow and white chrysanthemums, she asked him if he still loved Beth.

'Do you . . . you know . . . still feel the same way about her? *Love* her, I mean?'

'More than ever. Much more. More and more and more. Every year -- *more*.'

They walked through what was left of the night dew, and at the door of her hotel they paused. The reception area was deserted; too early even for the stern proprietress.

'Look,' Tess said timidly, not looking into his eyes, 'you won't be *embarrassed* about confiding in me, will you? You know I'd *die* rather than ever mention anything that passed between us tonight.'

'*Last* night now.' He smiled at her, but his mouth had a tightness. 'Your lips are sealed,' he teased. But hung about at her door. Then the thought came to her to acknowledge her own downtrodden desire. Why not? Why not ask him up? Ask him up to room 33 with the creaking bed and the man coughing through the wall? She turned to him. The instinct to ask him up sat there between them, solid and demanding as hunger or the need to have a good cry. Perhaps she would comfort him. Perhaps they would be shriven; making love in a welter of tears. But, no, she is a bit too proud. It is that woman wiping around the bath in London he wants. It is not her. But she would so like just a little piece of the mud of passion he was nostalgic for. She would be, like that drawing in the old pornographic book she had found in a stall by the Seine, '*The Cossack's Plaything*'. She would be like that naked woman on the Cossack's knee. A toy; a diversion after battle. 'Well, I must sleep,' she announced to his inscrutable waiting face. Perhaps it had never occurred to him that she might do otherwise. But he looked worried now. She knew he would be, because he had entrusted her with his secret. He had given a slip of a girl power over him. He had trusted her. Like those French 15-year-olds she had heard about who had been chosen by the SOE to cycle at night to the German Panzer tanks and pour sugar into their petrol tanks, immobilizing the whole division; shifting the balance of the war. Young people were braver. It was a famous paradox. They had more to lose and they were braver. Why had that older woman Paul had loved, that lucky Beth creature, allowed her husband to conduct her life; issue ultimatums? It was *vieux-jeu*. It was being a doormat. She was probably going to spend the rest of her life weeping, wailing and gnashing her teeth, making everyone around her miserable.

Tess was far off the mark. Beth and Tom still lived, comparatively content, in the same old house in Holland Park. There had indeed been periods when the house no longer seemed warm and welcoming; when flowers were left to fill the room with the smell of their own death; tea-towels remained unwashed; the bath unwiped. Beth's occasional depressions were put down to the menopause. Tom had given up girls because one tried to commit suicide. Even light love was dangerous and deep. He often came home to an empty fridge, but uncomplainingly went out to the take-away shops that were beginning to proliferate in the area. He knew that it was all part of his punishment; but he knew also that it would pass like everything else. And he could still make Beth laugh; take off her glasses and laugh herself young again. She had too broad an imagination, too much interest in the world to be completely felled by a broken heart. Anyway, as she told herself, at least she knew now what love poetry was all about. Like the sea, she had measured her depths. But she quaked at the thought of ever seeing Paul again.

# TEN

Tess, bored and lonely, watched the rain splash on to the bullet-ridden wall. The *boulangerie* opposite was unlit, sombre, this being a fête day; for which saint she wasn't quite sure, but someone had said St Vitus – could that be possible? Then it would be a day of madness. A student played pinball with spite and violence and the barman polished glasses. Polished without looking at them. He could do it blindfold.

The coffee machine burst into hisses and the telephone rang and rang. Maybe it was her mad mother tracking her down. Well, at least someone cared about her. Paul had been avoiding her for weeks, although just the other day he had looked at her with an odd, questioning expression as if after all he was prepared to acknowledge that night. But it was bound to be her mother, in a state as usual. She felt a rush of warmth towards her, despite that messy childhood; being uprooted from Lausanne when she had a daily routine, friends at school, a pet dog; when everything was charged with meaning. Afterwards there was Rome, Tangier, and Paris, then hastily back to Rome. Always Mother escaping a lover. In each city Tess had a new school uniform, a new language had to be learnt, and although she inhaled languages like oxygen she exhaled them with the same ease. In all her travels she tidied up after her mother. She became adept at murderous letters (murder by letter, she thought of it).

'Darling,' her mother would beg. 'Write to Philippe/Josef/ Raoul. Explain it's over. Tell him to go away in your inimitable style – brief, tough, no room for negotiation.'

Yes, she had been given responsibility early in life; looking after Mother between lovers. Perhaps it gave her a certain expression, a set of the mouth that Paul had recognized when he first saw her in this café, which made him employ her; which made him confide in her; which made him walk away afterwards although she was dying for some love.

The telephone was still ringing, on and on. At last the waiter languidly answered it; then jerked it in her direction.

'*Il y a un type qui veut parler avec la tricoteuse anglaise.*'

It was not Mother. It was Paul on the line, from the Embassy. 'Look, sweetie, this is very very urgent. Meet me outside the Embassy as soon as you can. I'll be waiting. But do hurry because I've got a plane to catch.' He seemed to be panting.

The bastard. Cuts me for weeks, then whistles; and look how I scamper.

Because of the efficiency of the Métro system she arrived in less than half an hour. Paul was not waiting for her at the gates. It was raining badly. The courtyard was flanked with guards in rain capes, so she stood opposite under the awning of designer showrooms. Women went in and out, wearing clothes the like of which she would never possess; some with real jewels, interesting hats. As they aged, their accoutrements became more gorgeous. It was a form of compensation perhaps. But if they all stripped naked, then and there in the rain, they would be the humble ones.

Yes, Paul had avoided her after their night in Montparnasse. Avoided her, the bastard. Or, if they were forced to meet between her arrival to babysit and their departure, he was

guarded, polite, seldom looking at her, never joking as of old.
He had evidently regretted his indiscretion. He had become,
as she had so sorely predicted, *embarrassed.*

How could she have hoped otherwise? Wasn't he English,
tight-arsed, over-educated, wary, ambitious? Oh yes, very
ambitious. He had to keep the servant in her place, keep her
mouth shut by some kind of subtle intimidation.

She felt aggrieved, waiting there in the rain. But only last
week she had noticed him looking at her in a different way,
a little wryly, as if he wished at last to acknowledge what
had occurred between them. Had she passed the loyalty test
by not spilling the beans? Was she about to be tested again;
or what?

One of her shoes was leaking again, it was always the
left shoe that let in the rain. What *could* this summons
be about? Alison was out of town with the baby visiting some relative in Switzerland, so it couldn't be about
that. Could he perhaps want to apologize for being so
cold and standoffish lately? What an odd, imperious way
he had of going about it. Perhaps he wanted to declare
his love?

Paul ran across from the Embassy holding a grip and
wielding a large manila envelope. He talked rapidly under
the dripping awning, swivelling his eyes around like radar
as if suspecting he was under surveillance. He handed her
the manila envelope. 'The key's inside. And money for your
taxi. Take out the letter addressed to Alison and leave it on
the mantelpiece in front of the clock. It's got to be done
immediately because she'll be back tomorrow, quite early.
Leave the key beside it.'

'You're going. You're really going?' She spoke slowly as
if in a stupor.

He gave her a tired smile. The smile of exhaustion and
happiness. 'I can't live without Beth, you see. I tried. But

I can't do it.' He gripped her shoulder and she reached up a hand and covered his.

'Shouldn't you tell Alison yourself? Shouldn't you . . . '

He broke away and shot across the road, hailing a passing taxi; threw his grip in the back seat and got inside, rolling down the window. He looked at her for the last time, put his finger to his lips, miming 'sssshhhh'.

Through the back window he gave one slight wave of the hand, then sank back out of sight. He knew she would do what he asked. It was an easy enough errand, but there were kids who would mess it up. Not her. He had to believe that. Otherwise he couldn't leave town. And he must. Must. No more procrastinating until the last moment. This *was* the last moment. When would Alison leave Paris again? It could be months, years. And there was one thing he knew about himself for certain: he could not face female pain.

Tess hailed a second taxi, asking it to go to Paul's place; paid the driver with the cash he had given her. She stood for several minutes outside his flat after ringing the bell, waiting, in case Alison had come home early from her trip. It was not unknown for her to break short her rare visits elsewhere, returning early, displaying her naked dependence, driving Paul mad.

Tess took the key from the envelope and let herself in. Queasily she went into the *salon*. The room seemed to quake with the possibility of outrage, alarmed discovery – its shutters were open, curtains undrawn, letting in witnessing eyes from the hotel on the corner.

But the door did not burst open to reveal Alison holding a gun, asking what the hell she was up to, wrenching the document out of her grip, rushing to the airport, stopping everything from happening that had to happen at last.

If Alison *should* appear, she would say – she would say she had lost some knitting pattern or perhaps a skein of Angora wool of a particular shade; but how would she explain having the key? That was what worried her. Alison would think she'd had one cut without asking and would suspect her of all sorts of felonies: letting herself into the flat to dress up in her clothes, perhaps; using the flat for orgies with her disreputable friends; or, worse, having trysts there with Paul. Alison must have noted how she gazed at him. How could Paul have overlooked this possibility? The dam must have burst before he could organize his escape with his normal aplomb.

It was by dwelling on her own momentary discomfort should she bump into Alison (before the deed was done) that gave her the courage to cross the room. She left the sealed envelope, as her master had instructed, on the mantelpiece, propped up against the eighteenth-century clock. The white rectangle shone where she placed it, supported by the breasts of a Greek goddess. But which one? The creature was winged. It could be Nemesis. It was the same kind of clock for which de Gaulle's aunt had sewn a gauze brassière to conceal the deity's breasts.

She could guess only too well the horror the letter contained. *Brief, tough, with no room for negotiation.*

That night she found it hard to sleep but, after taking some aspirins, managed to enter muzzy oblivion.

'Mademoiselle, *mademoiselle.*'

Tess jerked up from the bottom of an abyss; from the jumble of a dream (knitting dozens of absent fathers while an oyster held the wool); sat up in the pitch dark of her hotel room, sick to the stomach, heart thudding.

The man next door also sat up and commenced a spate of accusing coughs; her neighbour had only just managed to drop off himself, and the moon had already come and gone, leaving the surviving stars always there at their posts like grim old aunts.

She fumbled out of a knot of scratchy blankets and opened the door, shivering. Madame, who was also the maid, the manager and the night porter, stood in the traditional stained dressing gown, slippers and hair-curlers.

'*Il est quatre heures du matin!*' she accused.

'Oh, *pardon*, madame.' Tess took full responsibility for the hour of the hyena, clasping her cheek with remorse.

'*Téléphone. Urgent.*'

She followed madame down the stairs, nightdress billowing in draughts, feet chilled on lino. It couldn't be Alison. It wasn't dawn yet. Please God it's not Alison in a state of hysteria, Paul's letter clutched in her hand. No, no, at this time of night it must be Mother. Aurora in maudlin mood; regretting one of her lovers or temporarily foiled in her strategy to acquire another.

Tess took the call behind the reception area. Madame had had to climb six flights to get her. Not every old lady would have bothered. She could, if just a bit meaner or more fatigued, have let the phone ring itself to death.

'Well, what is it, Mother? Are you all right? There's such a din. Are you in a night club?'

'Am I speaking to Tess?'

It was a man's voice. A stranger's voice. In the background there was a roar as if he was at a street carnival, except there was no note of merriment.

'Sorry to wake you at this hour. But it is very urgent.'

An unfamiliar and terrible chill possessed her.

'You're a friend of Paul Radcliffe, aren't you?'

'Yes.'

'Can you get into their flat? Have you got the key? Or can you make the concierge open the door?'

'I've got the key.'

'Ah . . . ' For a while the man was silent, as if with intense relief. More roars in the background. A clatter of typewriters. A hellish perturbation. Who was this emissary from hell?

'I thought you might have left it on the mantelpiece, with the letter.'

'I forgot.' Her voice was trembling. 'Who are you?'

'My name's Tom Scrutton. Look, there's been an accident. Paul's plane crashed on its way to Marseilles. He was on his way to meet my wife. They were running away together.'

Tess giggled, but pulled herself together by staring at a poster of Serge Reggiani, the singer all Paris loved. His latest song came into her head. She hummed a few notes of it: all Paris nodded wisely to the words, about the woman in his bed who hadn't been 20 for a long time and whose eyes were circled by too many years.

It occurred to her, in sudden rage, that Serge Reggiani also hadn't seen 20 for a long time – and his eyes were also deeply circled by an even greater number of years.

Recognizing shock, Tom explained in a gentler voice that he and his wife were each other's best friends. She had got him to agree that this time she must do what she wanted, even though the decision to go, when it came, was so sudden. It was a kind of relief all round.

'Paul finally decided to seize the moment before his wife returned. You know . . . men are cowards ever!'

'Are they?'

Paul had been writing to Beth every day and he had referred to a regular babysitter who lived in the area, named Tess. For the last hour or two teams of journalists had been ringing every hotel on the Left Bank asking to speak to an English girl named Tess and had found her at last. (He had not, of course, told the staff the reasons for it all because it was top secret.)

'This is top secret, Tess. Now and for always.'

She thought of dynamite exploding under an eighteenth-century clock. She could see the intricate works bursting apart, embedding in the walls like shrapnel.

'What do you want me to do?'

'That letter . . . '

'How do you . . . ?'

'Now look. You must destroy that letter. And don't leave the key behind. A husband intending to return from a routine business trip – for that is what Alison now must believe – takes his key.'

'Alison is coming back any minute.' Tess was panicking.

'You can do it. You've *got* to get there before she does. No point in her knowing he was leaving her *now*, is there? No point at all. Is there, Tess?'

No point. No point in having a broken heart for nothing.

Tom explained that he had already phoned Beth, who had arrived at the meeting point in Marseilles. The lovers had been going to get tomorrow's ship for Casablanca.

It was ridiculous. It was like an old movie. She thought she was going to vomit.

'I had to break the news before she heard it on the radio or in a newspaper.' The story (story?) had come in on the teleprinters just before midnight; the plane had crashed somewhere south of Lyons, somewhere in the hills of Provence, in a field of lavender.

'So you see, Tess. And you are the one he most trusted. He told Beth that. He told her he had let his hair down with you one night; sort of snapped.'

It was bound to happen, yes, after all those years of bottling it up. The bottle exploded; some of the bits of glass got lodged into her. And then later, when he withdrew, she was so circumspect. She did not ogle him with her knowledge. She was good, loyal; trying to earn his love the slow way.

'He's dead?'

Tom did not reply for a moment. He had had hours to digest this news. He had to fly out now and rescue Beth; draw her back into the fold, under the army greatcoat of Welsh protection; clear the debris. And swear Tess to silence. For what was the point of needless pain? You would only want to spread it about if you were filled with malice.

'So he's dead then? Paul?'

She kept prodding the silence. Madame had stopped glaring. Perhaps she recognized the meaning of the word 'dead'.

'Everyone on board died immediately. The story will be headlines in every newspaper. You must hang up, go out and get that letter now. Before Alison returns. We are wasting time.'

She hung up and thanked madame, who nodded with a sad, lopsided smile of commiseration. She ran back to her room, releasing a new onslaught of coughs. She put on trousers, plimsolls and two woollen jumpers (as yet unsold).

As she ran up the road tulips on balconies bulged at her from their sockets. Starlight crept down on all fours, helpful, but not enough, like perfunctory love. She almost stepped on a *clochard* sleeping above air vents. How could he sleep so deeply without a blanket covering him? The question nagged her until she arrived at the Count's mansion. She pressed the buzzer for the second time that night, the door clicked open, and for a second time she feared the concierge. But there was no commotion, no tweak of the curtains. She continued over flagstones and crunching gravel until she arrived at the staircase, which creaked more than last time. If challenged, she would bluff her way through like spies parachuted into France landing in a sea of parachute-silk and being met by the wrong hands.

At the front door she could not work the key in the lock except by holding one wrist with her other hand like a marksman. What a coward she was. How bad she would have been in the front line. But it still didn't open the door. Then she remembered that in Paris keys work the wrong way.

When it opened at last she crept into the dark, turning into the *salon*, stiff with fright. Dawn filtered through, turning the room spectral. The envelope loomed with a terrible whiteness, its edges crisp as razors, *Alison* scrawled across it in Paul's faithless hand. Tess pocketed it and turned away to go. But in the hall she hesitated. Tom Scrutton had not thought of everything.

She went up to check Paul's study. It had two skylights, and up there it seemed the sun was rising, gilding the room. She looked around: furniture all in place; nothing incriminating. There was the bed in which he slept when they were estranged, or when he was too busy with work to stand Grizelda's crying, or when he simply didn't feel like the desperate expectations of the marriage bed – occasions which had occurred almost nightly in the past few months, but which Alison would shortly expunge from her mind as soon as she began her career as Paul's widow.

Tess opened the cupboard. His clothes hung there. It was packed. Perhaps he meant to send for his things later, after Alison got over the blow, when the time came for solicitors and legal questions.

As she had suspected, there was something too neat about the place; too final looking. Things looked ready for the shipping agency to send in the packers, with none of the loose ends and unexplained items always left when people die without preparation. Why had he waited to write the letter in the Embassy? Was he frightened she might find it before he left; frightened she would do one of her boring early returns? He was a great one for the *coup d'état* when the back was turned; the *fait accompli*.

Tess took out his coat and draped it over the back of the chair. When the concierge turned off the heating at night he often put it on as he worked at his desk. It would seem quite natural for him to leave it there if he had only popped down to Marseilles on business. But why Marseilles? This would niggle Alison; niggle at her mind. Wouldn't she ask them to explain it at the Embassy? Or would she let it go, assuming it to be something confidential? It was normal for diplomats to do a bit of routine spying. They all did it. She had learned not to ask questions. She would let it disappear into the void of things best forgotten, like the sexlessness of their marriage bed recently. Tess took the broken umbrella out of the bin and put it under his desk. She took books out of shelves and scattered them about, leaving some open, like the dictionary and one volume of the *Encyclopaedia Britannica*.

Stealthily, she went downstairs and made a cup of tea using the teapot Paul had always used, and the Jackson's Orange Pekoe he ordered from Fortnum's. She set the tray, adding a plate of his favourite lady-fingers, and took it back upstairs. She sat at Paul's desk and opened Paul's file, spreading out the papers, giving them an impression of having been recently toiled over. She sat there, gulping tea, the spoon clanking like the rattle of chains in a haunted house.

She opened the bottom drawer of the filing cabinet and extracted the expensive Havana cigars. She tried to smoke one, but doubled up with a coughing fit; she stubbed it out fiercely, bending it in two. She munched a biscuit, preparing the fake evidence that Paul had only gone away for a night, not for ever and ever; not for all eternity; covering for Paul until the light sparkled on her hair and the central heating began its morning clicking. The concierge was definitely up and in the basement now, turning on the heating, which was syphoned off to the Count's mansion from the public incinerators.

The clicking scared her. She hurried downstairs and left the house, walking swiftly past the concierge's lodge. The gods had stayed with her so far, why should they abandon her now? They had punished Paul enough. They were famous for small mercies, not big ones.

At the corner she started to run, past the plaque to the Resistance hero, beneath the railings of the gardens, where leaves of espaliered pears poked through as if pleading for a wilder life. Cafés were filling with men downing brandies, and two dustmen in overalls were looking at an abstract painting of mystifying obscurity in the window of a chic little gallery. '*Pas mal,*' said one dustman, resting ruminatively on his broom. A classic Cartier Bresson. She should take her camera with her everywhere. Why did she always forget? Her mind was a fluff-ball.

At the Pont Neuf she stopped and looked over the edge. She had to wait for a vagrant to wander off. Cars were building up, a wall of witnesses to any mugging or rape, but the drivers would never notice a thing like a white letter, a lethal weapon jettisoned into the Seine. She took it out of her pocket, held it concealed in her fist, dangling that arm over the side of the bridge. She looked behind her at the waking world: the innocent tourists starry-eyed about Paris; mooning over love or money. She let the murderous letter drop. A wind blew it around and then shoved it back under the bridge in the direction of the Préfecture.

To make certain it had truly gone, she ran across the road. Cars hooted at the sallow girl in the raincoat with stringy hair. One driver shouted, '*Espèce de connasse . . .* ' She bent so far over the edge some thought it was an imminent suicide, someone taking the traditional way out, about to utter their final cry that would haunt them, but some selfish force kept them clutching the wheel. They would not be implicated, these guilty bystanders.

But after a few moments she straightened up and walked briskly back to the Place St-Michel, apparently sane after all. She had seen the letter drown slowly, but utterly, like Ophelia. It collapsed in the middle, a gleaming circle of water drew it downwards, innocent as a paper boat in the wake of a passing *bateau-mouche*.

She hadn't bothered to rip open its innards. She knew what the letter contained. Rejection, desertion, grief. She'd written enough of them for her *femme fatale* mother in her time. However nicely they were phrased, or with whatever guilty anguish, they were full of someone's blood.

Going back up the boulevard she said goodbye to the poster advertising Vittel, with its picture of the *bon père de famille* with the balloon coming from his mouth: '*Mon foie? Connais pas.*'

It had once been deeply mysterious. 'My liver? Don't know.' What was the meaning of it, she had wondered all those months ago when she first arrived. Now she knew what it meant. It meant: I don't have liver problems because I drink Vittel mineral water. There he sat, the *bon père*, presiding over the *quartier* with a self-satisfied smirk, patting his paunch – a corpulence concierges would admire because it proved him to be a gourmet with a *bon appétit*. Goodbye, goodbye, goodbye. She was sick of all this French stuff. She would leave Paris. And not come back.

# AURORA

## *1991*

*Ah, could the memory cast her spots, as do*
  *The snake's brood theirs in spring! and be once more*
*Wholly renew'd, to dwell i' the time that's new . . .*

Earl of Lytton, *A Night in Italy*

# ELEVEN

That was him, that old fisherman, covered in skin cancer, staggering a little, a little drunk, along the front of the port that evening. A tear almost rolled into Aurora's Campari. One great, rusty tear; but she held it back. He had been so eager a quarter of a century ago; he had sprung at the chance of earning a pound or two to take them out the next morning when he laid his nets. They would, of course, have preferred to see him haul them in, leaping with mullet and swordfish. But that occurred at the end of the day and they would be gone before tomorrow evening.

They had rowed out along the edge of the islands in the glaring morning sun. She had been a little bored, if she remembered rightly. But occasionally he had pointed out the whereabouts of a cormorant or a school of dolphins.

On the way back into harbour they had been hailed by an English lord on his cruiser and invited up, excluding the fisherman of course. He had been left in his bobbing boat while they had tea (served by nautical lackeys) and stilted conversation. Philippe was too dapper and foreign to appeal much to milord. But her glamour lulled him. They were merely a ball of wool to an elderly cat. Amusing for a quarter of an hour, no more.

They climbed back into the waiting boat, helped by the

fisherman, who then rowed them back to shore, his sunburnt arms pulling steadily, his eyes full of the sea. That was all there had been to it. It wasn't as if they had spoken in broken languages. It wasn't as if he had been desirable.

So why this propensity for tears? Lipari had improved over the years. Tourism had cheered the place up, for once, instead of destroying it. Hydrofoils arrived regularly and there were lively restaurants and boutiques. Even the cats were fat. No longer those skinny Mediterranean wrecks.

She and Philippe had woken at five to meet him, just over there, by the dented railings. He had caught her hand as she jumped in the boat; or had they waded through the shallows and stepped in unaided? She was a bit blurred about the details. Perhaps it wasn't even the same fisherman. Perhaps it was one of the others who were gathered by the chapel on the port laughing together, doubtless at the endless folly of tourists whom, at the same time, they had to placate.

She looked into her Campari. Her mind marshalled her emotions: You are weeping not for the fisherman, my pet. No, you are weeping for yourself; you are weeping about time and its dirty work.

The fisherman was capering now, all by himself, by the dented railing. At least the *railing* hadn't changed much. She could hold on to that. Such odd things the brain stored. It had even remembered that dent in the railing.

Game old ladies hurl themselves into gardening, archaeology or grandchildren – those hostages to fortune; more Stradivariuses with which life can display its evil ingenuity. Wallowing in self-pity is the great temptation for the old. For the young, it is wallowing in pity, and telling lies (though there had always been truth in *her* lies). Lying becomes less attractive with age. It is the truth that makes the heart beat faster, the breathing deepen, the cheeks blanch and blush.

'At present, you know, I'm suffering from a crisis of confidence. It's a nice phrase, isn't it?'

Gogol, a man with white hair and an excess of tolerance, ordered her another drink. 'We are the only generation since the amoeba split that had to please our parents *and* our children,' he said. 'Nobody has ever tried to please *us*. Except, of course, those paid to do so.'

The waiter arrived with the Camparis, beaming with joy. These two spent money. He had been right not to close up for the winter.

'I don't think my daughter cares if I live or die. So long as I visit her at Christmas. So long as I don't preach or interfere. So long as I don't, God help me, *ask* for anything.'

'Oh, I think Tess is fond of you, in her own peculiar way.'

She looked at Gogol affectionately. How remote he was from this place; he was just gliding through the holiday as usual, his mind on his work. What he seemed to like best, what made him most comfortable, was buying her things. It seemed natural to him. It was what he was used to. He had been married to a real Jewish princess and he was quite disconcerted by Aurora's own lack of acquisitiveness.

In fact Aurora was acquisitive, but for experiences, not things. She was greedy for life, for passion, for jokes, revelations that changed greyness into Technicolor. She sighed and sipped.

There was one thing deeper than love, sexual love, love for a man. There was one thing that could sweep you to further lengths and about which no one had ever given her the slightest warning. There had been all the warning in the world about what sexual passion could do. All those books that had lined her adolescent mind like icons, beaming their reassuring messages of inexhaustible depths, *coups de foudre*, dark entanglements, mysterious forces that both wrecked lives and created life. But for mother-love there had been no Tolstoy, no Brontë, no Lawrence. And when it had hit her, thirty-six years ago, it had done so with the unexpected force of a volcano, like Vulcana, should it erupt, that island they could see in the distance, steam pouring out of its sides.

No one had warned her, that was the thing she couldn't get over. Oh, she had been warned about the *difficulties* all right; the newspapers and magazines had been full of them – the boredom of being stuck at home with toddlers, the lack of intellectual companionship, the horrors of rebellious teenagers and post-natal gloom. No one had written about that feeling after birth when you understand the Renaissance madonnas. You know what celestial joy is.

And now her only child Tess lived in Suffolk with some dreary mate and hadn't written for weeks. She never answered letters. She disappeared for ages when she was 18; went to live in Paris – *pouf*. It was as if all that depth of feeling had never existed. And yet, after all, it was the bricks, the solid bricks under the personality. Whatever thunderstorms came after, whatever ghastliness. The loved child could sustain it, bear the future without crumbling. Unless of course, things got too bad. Aurora crossed herself in public.

'The trip's been a success, hasn't it? Except for the people we met. Too dull for you, my darling,' said Gogol, patting her, sensing her mood correctly as usual.

She tried him on her theory about motherhood being the great unwritten topic; at least its positive aspects. 'No, no, a much more interesting great unwritten topic is penises. Women who rage (in their macro-mini-skirts) at the perfidy of males should they react sexually should be condemned to inhabit the body of a 15-year-old boy for a single day.'

'But why don't chaps write about it? Din it into our heads?'

'Men are the demure sex, my love. They don't enjoy writing in the newspapers about the anarchic beast between their legs. So women are under the impression they can tame them.'

Before they left Sicily for the next stage of their tour, they managed to squeeze in a visit to a small hill town whose only tourist attraction was situated in the church vault: rotting bodies of seventeenth-century Sicilians dressed in seventeenth-century clothes. The skeletons still had shreds and patches of leathery flesh, one with his neck encircled by a dirty ruff and with skeletal feet shod in gold-buckled shoes that had outlasted him with hideous poignancy. Looked at long and hard enough, it would put an end to any possibility of believing in immortality, even when listening to Mozart.

# TWELVE

## New Year's night

Foggy night and a full moon. On the saloon deck of – the cross-channel ferry a man was staring at Aurora. She concentrated on her newspaper. But in the plate-glass over the poster of Mont-Saint-Michel his reflection glimmered into her lowered eyelashes; his smile undulating with the vibrations of the engine and the violent rocking of the ship. It was early on New Year's Eve. But there was no one else in the restaurant except the waiters, Gogol, herself and him, the stranger, a few tables away leaning against the porthole lashed by rain. The moon jerked in and out of view behind him.

Suddenly the ship lurched; cutlery skidded along the floor making waiters giggle and whoop. But no one had forgotten the recent cross-channel ferry disaster and there was an undertow of alarm in the giggles. The man went over and handed them back some dropped cutlery. Gogol rummaged about for his sea-sickness pills, his face looking lined and pouched. The effort of keeping up his gallantries aged him. He had the rubber face of an actor smiling out into the dark of an emptying auditorium. 'I'm going to find a cabin and lie down for a while.'

The stranger, leaning back against the porthole, was observing them as if they were in a play. It was more

99

amusing perhaps to watch them than the television blasting out vapidities on the other deck. Aurora turned away, severing the eye-line. Men still tried to pick her up on public transport. She had firmly resisted the most recent temptation. On her way to Suffolk to see Tess, a man on the train, engorgement in his eyes, had pressed a piece of paper with his telephone number on it into her hand. For a long time she imagined meeting him at a hotel she knew near Tess's house, where the great beam from the lighthouse swept with the regularity of a heartbeat across the double bed in room 3. But after some days of unrest she tore it up and threw it to the winds. The man could have been just anybody, a murderer perhaps. And besides, she loved her Gogol. She was going straight now.

She hunched lower over her newspaper but soon began to feel paralysed down the side closest to the man. She often wondered if cows felt like this when a bull entered the field and stood behind them, out of vision, but emitting a gale of irresistible testosterone. Once, standing in a theatre lobby, she had felt it from a man behind her. He was not handsome or rich or even very nice. Moreover, he was bald. But he had been her lover for two years and when he was fast asleep, his face softened in repose, she had loved the person he could have been before life twisted him up.

But for some time now she had wondered if that kind of impromptu adventure was a thing of the past.

She knew that today she was looking good. It was one of her young days. She could feel it by the lightness of her face. For the last two weeks on this long holiday she had been looking outwards, outwards at the world – Palermo, Lisbon, Paris – and it was filling her with lightness and light. And here she was, sitting so still and demure, and it was that old moth-candle stuff again. And *him* – fluttering into the scorch area.

The lower part of her eyes filled with darkness. She lifted her lids. It was his black coat. Him. Leaning over her. Fluttering a newspaper in her face. 'Can I borrow the *Independent*?'

She handed him the newspaper silently. He took it and, after a brief time, standing hovering over her averted head, her unforthcoming speech, he returned to his table.

She picked up a book, holding her head behind it as from an east wind, and pretended, even with a stiff neck, to read. Soon he came trotting over again with the newspaper.

'Not a bad paper.' He waited. She still said nothing. 'Wonderful, wasn't it, the way it sprang up out of the rubble, just when all the others seemed to have gone rotten?'

He watched her. She remained silent, averting her eyes.

'I've just nipped over to Paris for a friend's wedding,' he continued. His voice was pleasant, but there was a touch of deprivation in it. 'Have *you* been in Paris?'

'Just passing through.'

'I always pass through when I can. People say, "What do you see in that dump? The Parisians are so cold and mean and the traffic is hell. And what do you do there anyway?" And I say, "I *look*!"'

She felt her gills open. What was his name? He had a stocky frame, a square face, dark eyes and peasant hands. She could imagine him dancing boisterously at a harvest fête in some hill town in Transylvania before Europe was torn to pieces, and yet he had that London voice.

He would make love, she sensed, silently and straight-forwardly but with self-loathing if the act didn't come up to scratch. What did he do? Why was he on his own? Was he a bad penny, a bad egg; or, worse, a melancholic, a manic-depressive who in his manic phases could pick up pretty women and then react, immobile for weeks on end, picking away at the table-edge with stubby, despairing fingers? People could cast these nets of enchantment over each other when they first met, and the nets would be filled with their leaping fantasies. Knowledge of someone was another matter, it involved a slow climbing up of the dusty hillside, an acceptance of negative moods, inadequacies, inappropriate outbursts. She knew all that intellectually.

A young woman lurched into the tilting restaurant. It was New Year's Eve after all. Camaraderie was the order of the evening, even though midnight would strike when they were all back in England.

The girl invited them to look at her catalogue of recent French painters. 'Now this one is a Buddhist,' she said, turning the pages. How delightfully young she was. Aurora supposed the man would switch his attentions now. 'He has no sense of the political realities,' the girl informed them. 'There is no awareness in this picture of the sexist-racist question.'

Aurora looked slyly at the man.

'All paintings don't have to be agitprop,' he said, getting another mark from her.

When Gogol emerged from the cabin, yawning, to claim her, he saw the three people immersed in the catalogue of some modern French shit. But for one moment, one split-second, he paused, an animal in a forest sensing danger; then his rational self reassured him. He nodded to Aurora's pick-ups and gathered her and their baggage ready for disembarkation.

As they waved farewell Aurora felt relief. She had avoided trouble, perturbation of the heart. Doubtless the man would now turn his attention to the young art-lover. They lost them in the swarms of people going down the gang-plank.

Because of the disruption to the train service by New Year's Eve and foul weather the company had laid on buses to take them to other railway stations. Aurora and Gogol trudged across the damp port towards one of the many vehicles. They had been some time having their passports cleared and the buses were almost all full up.

Crossing the dark, wintry tarmac she looked up at the strange New Year moon under scudding clouds and found herself looking into the eyes of her Transylvanian peasant. He was staring down at her from the top window of one of the packed buses. Her mouth shimmered back at him into a glorious smile; and in the smile was delight and conspiracy. That smile had won the hearts of all waiters in all hotels she had ever passed through, and tonight it had the extra energy of release. He laughed down at her, safely glittering at her from above, through darkness and through rain, those classic footmen of romance.

They were taken in the last bus, under an on-off moon, to a distant station. It was even darker and foggier in there, and the indicator on the platform didn't seem to be operating. No one seemed to know when the train was due. Dark, badly lit stations had bad memories for both of them. Gogol slumped by the wall, his clown's face collapsing. Aurora's pick-up on the ship slid into the oblivion of fantasies. They were in the real world now.

'We should have brought the car. Just because you can't stand long drives . . . ' Gogol burst out, unable to bear standing at the station waiting for a train that might never come; standing like a stupid old sheep. 'I'm going to find someone in charge.' He stormed off through the crowd, all shuffling and waiting, breathing mistily, sheep waiting for the slaughter. She watched him tenderly as he barged through them all. She was used to his volte-faces.

Up and down the platform she strolled, shivering, watching the clouds, choppy as the Channel; the hectic moon made her want to bay.

When she turned, there was her shipboard romance, just standing there as if he'd dropped down in front of her from a cloud. He handed her a slip of paper. 'Give me a ring some time,' he muttered.

'Maybe I will,' she said with archaic coyness, a strand of hair slipping over her eye, noticing with a kind of shame the huskiness and conspiracy in her voice.

# THIRTEEN

For some weeks she did nothing about it; nothing. It was stupid, adolescent; she had to grow up. But the piece of paper was secreted in her handbag in a special zip pocket intended for stamps. It beat like a second heart, it hummed like a song she could never switch off, it taunted, it pleaded, it whispered, it coaxed, then it retained a cogent silence.

One afternoon when Gogol was at his studio (because it was essential that Gogol never knew these things; he would go mad, become a wolf tracking her throughout the day and night, spying on her through window cracks, scrabbling at the bark of trees), she phoned him. Her new lover. He answered and her throat dried. Words filed out of her mouth like dunces. His voice had been waiting for her.

They arranged to meet the following Tuesday.

On Tuesday morning she called him from a phone box to cancel it. She told him Gogol had flu. It was the truth. But it could easily be a lie. She was frightened of meeting him anyway. He could be a lunatic or jail-bird. What did she know of him? He might smoulder his eyes at every woman on the cross-channel ferry every day of the week. Maybe that was his terrain; his turf.

Maybe he is some kind of con-man specializing in women of an age when they become a little insecure but usually have access to their husband's money. Women who need sexual reassurance, who won't notice if their money gets depleted in the process. She heard herself agreeing to meet him. Yes, she would see him next week. No, she would not let him down again.

Below the ripple of daily life, the nursing of Gogol, the telephone calls to cronies, the errands, there was now another great warm tide; a gulf stream warming up the ocean, affecting the migration of moods, the breeding of thoughts.

'You're a wonderful nurse,' Gogol said, tucking into his chicken and tarragon, looking forward to the next chapter of the Oscar Wilde biography; coaching her in her French when he could. It was still imperfect despite all her travels in France over the years. But he could see a certain shine on her that indicated she had something in store; a sense of acres of pine forests in her blood, untold possibilities. How young she looked, vivid and potent, full of future and health. Perhaps staying young was all a matter of self-belief.

Outside the Soho pub she braced herself. The winter had turned nasty and she feared her nose was red, her eyes watery. The moment she opened the door she saw him talking to someone else. But he turned away quickly and grabbed her by the upper arm, jolting electric currents through her body, leading her out again into the freezing night, into a razor-blade wind. Was he known in there? Would there be gossip about him which would not enhance his strategies with her? Why was he in such a rush to leave? It was crowded, but so was everywhere in the West End at this time on a winter's evening. It was the cheapest place to keep warm in.

As they toiled down towards Trafalgar Square he told her that he had been born in the smallest of the Scilly Islands. And a new glorious breadth came into her idea of him; surrounded by the shining circle of the sea; collecting shells; knowing the ways of sea birds. A man whose strength is as the strength of ten because his heart is pure.

As they walked along in the freezing night she held her arms stiffly so they wouldn't clutch hold of him with undue boldness. She was carrying a book by Elias Canetti, who used to hold court over coffee tables in Hampstead and who had inscribed the flyleaf for her, with a more than friendly message.

At last they found a pub that pleased him, because it was quiet. He ordered two bitters. She didn't ask for what she wanted – a gut-warming whisky or bloody mary – in case he quailed at the cost. His shirt had a frayed collar and was not ironed. He did not take off his coat. Perhaps he was afraid of revealing something: a paunch, perhaps. She hoped very much there was a paunch under the coat, something to balance the fact that she was much older than he; something that had to be firmly overlooked if there was to be romance. Something to equalize things.

He picked up the book in her hand and read the inscription to her. 'What are famous people like?' he enquired, making her melt at such naïvety.

She is careful not to stun him with the story of her life. It was so long. So complicated. It would be like having the entire *Encyclopaedia Britannica* fall on his head. Even the concise version would stun him; God knows.

He worked at the Albert Hall on a part-time basis: sometimes as an usher, sometimes in the bars. But he had an aptitude for French (probably Huguenot ancestry, she decided) and whenever he could he taught French to private pupils. He had only one pupil at present. It sounded a little bleak, his life.

She told him about her difficulties with French. Her

ambition had always been to speak it well. On her death bed she would still be trying to master the subjunctive. Her brain was a sieve as far as languages were concerned. This was very embarrassing because everyone expected her (so cosmopolitan) to speak languages fluently. It was thought to be compensation for having been uprooted, for having been flattened and disrupted like the great Anatolian plains.

'Well, here we are now, a little chip of the Scillies, a little chip of Vienna sitting together in a London pub,' he said. 'Why are we in a London pub and not in Paris, the city we both love? Because London is kinder, I think. And I was brought up here. It was a cramped sort of life, but decent.' Then his voice changed, became angry, almost hysterical. 'That was before the bestialization of the working classes by the tabloid newspapers.'

He seemed obsessed by something rotten in England to do with Mrs Thatcher and which took its vilest form in the *Sun*.

'The tabloids were always filthy,' she said.

'But have you read the *Sun* lately? You might just faint.'

She might faint? Did he think she was some shockable old duck? She went on upstairs to the Ladies room. Returning, she looked at him from a distance, and her face fell into sexual expectation. Their words were just pebbles that opposing armies throw at each other across a stream before the battle begins.

She looked at her watch. She must go, or Gogol would get suspicious. He walked her to the tube, kissing her on the mouth; his eyes open, searching her. 'You'll ring me, won't you?'

She had been frightened back there that she would talk too much, talk a wall around herself, talk away Eros; something she had done lately in situations that seemed to be coming to the boil; something to do with a new sense of the dignity appropriate to her age.

She forced herself to wait three days before making the second call. She stroked her body – a cold field whose buried seeds feel the intimation of sun. She tried to put him out of her mind. But dissonance, like certain chords in Shostakovich, felt real to her; felt satisfying. It was what she was used to on the emotional level. Living harmoniously with Gogol was Mozart and she loved Mozart. But dissonance; percussion and strings at each other's throats, that was what made her feel most alive, gave her that immortal feeling; gave her back her vigour.

Obsession began its old insistent beat, like birds in a tiny cage breaking their wings against the bars. *She must show some control.* He was in his early 40s. She was older, older. She didn't formulate her age exactly. She had no right to expect beauty, life, renaissance or the hooves of Pan. She should be sitting on the wall in black, knitting her past and her child's future. She should have no present other than to serve.

She noticed things she never noticed before; like the architectural detail of a certain building she walked by every day. Noticing things, she realized, was not just a matter of perspectives but of states of mind; states of emotion.

That night, in their flat, she noticed the dust; the grime around door handles.

This time, when she phoned him, they arranged to meet inside the British Museum. She looked in the mirror, at her own shining eyes. Her body, which she kept stroking, had a new hunting sleekness. To accept a conventional idea of what was seemly for one's age was to be no more developed than an impoverished, uneducated, overworked Bedouin woman. It was bowing to authority, misogyny and the stereotype; to hell with them all. She was different; always had been; locked in her alarming differences. Anyway, in his face she had seen desire. He was the furnace in the earth. They were made of the same stuff.

On Sunday afternoon, when Gogol was playing chess with Arnie, she lay on her bed looking at her face as it might seem to someone lying on top of her, or beside her. What she saw scared her, made her want to cry. At a cocktail party recently at least three people had told her she was gorgeous. Were they seeing something that was not in the mirror? Would her lover see the mirror-truth or the other-truth? Or had he seen something on the ship – the glow she always got from travelling? In his flat, one morning, maybe on the first morning, he would see only the cold facts of the mirror. Then her pain would begin.

The snow continued to fall. Freak snow; snow piled higher than anyone could remember. You had to wear boots to go out. She knew before looking in the mirror that it was one of her beautiful days. Was it just hormones, or something to do with the spirit as well? Or was it just the body-clock arriving at the harmonious moment when the hour, minute and second-hand were all in alignment . . . all pointing (today) towards the rendezvous.

Aurora laughed, getting dressed; a long thick skirt, a huge warm jumper decorated with a phoenix (one of Tess's first commercial successes) and these green Wellingtons. What a terrible day. But she would not put off the meeting. Perhaps he would put it off? After all, the snow, snow like this, a Switzerland in England, was a perfect excuse to cancel everything and anything; abort all dangerous meetings.

Before she left the house she heard the newsflash: there had been bombs in Westminster. The IRA or someone had tried to blow up Downing Street. Three missiles had been aimed at the heart of government, had sped across St James's Park, and one had almost hit the mark.

Gogol advised her against putting her nose out of doors.

She went out into a padded, silenced, world; falling snow had stopped traffic, renewed the dirty streets. There was a sense of collective shock; a gigantic hush as of the world listening at a keyhole. She had not experienced anything like it since 1968, when de Gaulle disappeared and she, visiting Paris with Raoul, walked through a city of abandoned cars, some upturned like beetles, looks of dawning terror on the faces of the occasional pedestrians weaving their way across the Place de la Concorde. A cyclist dressed in a dinner jacket off to some soirée, with all the nonchalance of wealth, waved to her over the debris. She had wanted to leave Raoul and jump on the back of his bike; sail over the debris with style; that was the stance she most admired in life.

Not since then had she felt this collective silence. The city was a great clock that had stopped ticking. Perhaps the tubes wouldn't work. It had been impossible to ask for Gogol's car in such weather, he would have remonstrated with her, pointing out the dangers of skidding. He would have been suspicious.

But the tubes were working, although there was no one using them. Even the snow piled at the entrance was still clean. Opposite her on the empty platform there was an Irish drunk. Just the drunk and herself out travelling that day: two desperadoes.

Inside the museum her island king greeted her; so dark against the snow piled against the glass windows. There seemed to be no colour anywhere. What a black and white world it was; but filled with a silvery light.

Because of the combination of freak snow and explosions there was no one about in the great halls of culture. Their footsteps echoed through room after room as in a dream. In front of the Assyrian kings he said, 'All this feels profoundly familiar.'

'Maybe you have a genetic memory; maybe your ancestors came trudging over the Urals then sailed to the remotest island they could find to escape persecution . . . Notice that sphinx, it's got the head of a man (mind), a horse's body (strength) and wings (ingenuity) . . . the perfect creature . . . ' She stopped suddenly, forcing herself to shut up. She would not blind him and bind him with one of her dizzy, headlong fantasies. They might amuse Gogol, but they would only perplex this boy, put him off. And above all she didn't want him to be put off.

In the Graeco-Roman section she found herself, for the first time in years, able to look at the Elgin Marbles without being crowded out. She stood back, dangling her handbag behind her, gazing up at the nostrils of a charging horse. Hands touched her waist and slid up to her breasts, which became two circles of fire. They were the barometers of her sexuality, either untouchable or inflammable. Maybe breast-feeding Tess for over a year had kept them so high and springy.

She turned and whispered, 'Just wanted to make sure it was really you.'

He dropped his hands. 'I didn't notice you objecting, even if it wasn't.' He sounded huffy. God, he was dull; chip-on-shoulder dull; she moved a few steps away, gazing unseeingly at a dying warrior.

But he followed her and kissed her very hard. When they unlocked she shuddered. 'I've got the shivers.'

He tried to push her against a wall but there were attendants somewhere and she thought she could hear distant but approaching footsteps.

'Come back to my place then,' he muttered, adjusting himself under his coat.

'I must go home. Gogol will be wanting dinner.'

Attendants watched with amusement as they left the museum holding hands. While she earnestly explained the absolute impossibility of staying any longer they hurried towards his council flat. He paused only once, to straighten a fallen bottle by a dozing tramp. She warmed to him for that.

Crossing St James's Park there was no one else in all the world; nor had there ever been. And the world consisted of the absolute whiteness of snow in the chill of dusk.

Ducks and geese were stranded on the iced-over lake and the frozen trees shone under the first stars. The smell of cordite hung in the air, rank as a poison-flower in the stillness. The waning moon shone down on snow. It was all hallucinatory, theatrical. She could not have hoped for such a magnetic evening.

He lived in a block in a back street. Going up in the horrible lift she looked at the floor, silent and afraid. Walking down the shabby corridor she wondered if she were seeking her own destruction. If there were not some taint of the murderee in her compulsions.

The moment they got inside, before he took off his coat he began to rip off her clothes, pushing her on the floor to take off her underwear. Over his shoulder she noticed the photograph of his grandmother in its frame on the wall and another photograph of fishermen mending nets. And there was one of a catamaran. But she was stiff, shy; not exactly ashamed of her body, which was slim enough, but *awkward*. It had been too long since she had played the game. She had forgotten the moves; forgotten how to dance. And he had pounced too soon.

He pulled her towards the bedroom and took off his own clothes in the dark. As she had predicted, he was a good, straightforward lover, but did it without relish – no style or gaiety. But, as she had hoped, he was a bit fat. This helped to soothe her. His eyes shone in the semi-dark as he laboured over her.

But the build-up had promised too much. The choppy sea, the full moon, the cross-channel ferry in the storm; the snow, the explosions; all the cinematic props. And perhaps she had been too shrewd; too silent, not revealing her true Central European gesticulating talkativeness, keeping that side of her down so that Prince Eros could triumph, could walk his domain in silence and majesty and, above all, darkness. If you burn too bright a light on him, he vanishes. Lamplight or intellectual light. This is the great ancient story of Cupid and Psyche. She had always known it. But how long could she subdue her true nature? She would not even have attempted to do so if the man had been her own age; but she knew how easy it would be to frighten him off if she showed him her real measure.

She looked up at his eyes, dark eyes, sad eyes, kind eyes, and said lightly (when it was all over and done with), 'Who the hell are you anyway?'

'That's a strange question,' he said, puzzled.

The man had no play in him. Maybe he was dim. The result of island inbreeding. Good, she would not fall in love with him. She was safe.

# FOURTEEN

When she returned to Belsize Park, Gogol was upset.
There had been a break-in. A window in their bedroom had been forced open, prying hands had tipped out her bureau drawers, pawed through her underwear, disdaining her trinkets which lay scattered everywhere. The intruder had taken nothing. Nothing. It was very odd. Perhaps he had been scared off by the approach of Gogol.

The break-in frightened her, chastened her; made her resolve never to see that man again. It was a warning from the gods; warning her of the chaos that could ensue after all unwise couplings. She was reminded of the desirability of peace and stability and the continuing support and affection provided by Gogol. The other stuff was vanity.

She blamed her excessive lateness on the bomb outrages, the freak snow which caused cancellation of trains and the disruption of buses and the disappearance of taxis; splendid excuses no one could possibly argue with.

She woke the next day determined to wipe the event out of her mind; that awkward adventure. She tried to think of other things. She went to the market and bought seeds for starving birds. She was amused when the old woman in front of her in the queue spoke of fairies she had seen on Hampstead Heath;

with wings and net dresses and wands, dancing in rings on blue grass. She would forget the man with the dark eyes and the twisted mouth. Leave him to his own inscrutable destiny. She bought two Dover soles for dinner.

Coming home with the fish and the birdseed, the word 'PASSION' leapt at her suddenly from a newspaper hoarding and sank into her body. It seemed to be related to some football event.

All afternoon she worked on her French. She made a list of all the words she had to look up when she tried reading Camus's *The Fall* in the French edition. Every word participated in her secret turmoil: *future, bonds, to belong, to put away again, to swear, embodied, oath, winning, a third, unforeseen, checkmate, failure, glittering, pleading, display, loss, as soon as, irritation, consent, recognition between a vassal and his overlord, number, nape of neck, concealed, shock, inform.* It was like an experimental novel abut her private life; every word loaded with too much meaning.

He did not phone. *He did not phone.* Even though she had told him it would be safe in the afternoons, when Gogol was at his studio.

The radio forecast another week of arctic weather, freezing fog, black ice on the road, with recommendations to local authorities to grit hazardous surfaces. Grit. Grit. She had not heard from him. No note. No call. She gritted her teeth and accepted she had been a flop, a failure, a one-night stand, erotically null and void. A rusty old moll who should be sitting on the village wall, knitting alongside her daughter, who always acted old and responsible even when she was a young filly with elastic limbs and a risky wide smile.

At the butcher's she met a neighbour who fancied herself as clairvoyant. She grabbed Aurora's hand and informed her that she was about to fall madly in love. 'And this time you're going to die of it.' Aurora escaped the woman in a welter of jokes about love having no value unless it leads to death.

She moved slowly through the hours. Every half-hour or so she would hear a distant explosion. Everyone was jumpy. Every half-hour it went on: *boom, boom, boom*. It went on for days. But it was only the noise of snow, great lumps of snow; disenfranchised snow falling from treetops and rooftops. Cannon-shots of snow. As it melted, these great white boulders hit the ground; bits of her heart hit the ground; bits of her self: *boom, boom, boom*.

In a dream she was a lean, sleek wolverine pelting ahead at great speed towards her prey, only to be hit by a lump of snow. The wolverine retired, shivering, under cover. Occasionally she would turn her head and lick fur, the gleam in her eye faltering, but not extinguished. Not yet extinguished. She was still in oestrus.

Aurora was still in oestrus of the mind. She walked through the days exhausted; exhausted, she supposed, by the arduous task of resignation. The sky hung low now, grey and incontinent as a decrepit old lady. It looked as if a storm would break out at last and clear the air, but day followed day and the prolapsed sky dropped only a few drops.

It had been a one-night stand. Perhaps he specialized in them. A Don Juan. He had arranged the full moon, the stormy sea, the dipping boat, the sea-sickness of Gogol. There was even a fog that night. All the cinematic props. To top it all he pretended he was a storm-tossed islander. No wonder her new-found matronly calm and dignity were disrupted, her pleasant resignation, in the ante-room of old age and sickness and death. She used to think obsessively about love; now she and Gogol thought obsessively about death; planning how they would kill each other if Alzheimer's struck, with all that vile humiliation.

How could she possibly have resisted the snow and the

cordite night? The birds on the frozen pond and the smell of explosions in the air? The word 'fate' came into her mind, but she dismissed it. Fate was another word for God, which implied that there was something inhabiting the centre of things. Nobody believed that now, no matter how much they yearned to, nobody with eyes to see how the world wagged.

In the evenings Gogol read out loud from *The Brothers Karamazov* – the chapter about children locked in cupboards, tormented by brutes. There was no reply whatsoever to that terrible diatribe. There could be no God if He allowed that, and to bleat of 'free will' didn't wash. Survivors of Auschwitz said you got to hate the sky, because the sky was empty.

Day followed day. Week followed week. The year dragged on. She received no message at the 'safe' hour in the mid-afternoon. She was a Rolls-Royce, her engine turned on full by expectation, but with the handbrake left on. All that throbbing energy had nowhere to go, except to wear out the engine. Her face became pouched, lined; her shoulders hunched.

'I'm sorry I'm so dull these days. I'm a bit depressed,' she told Gogol.

'It's the weather. Light deprivation.'

He bought her flowers the next day, bursting into the apartment with a huge bunch of white gladioli and a sheepish expression. She pulled herself together. She loved Gogol and told herself to grow up; to drop her dark side, to give it to Oxfam along with her stilettos and other out-of-date glad-rags.

Soon her looks improved, and although she was too thin there was harmony once more in her bearing; beauty. But in the mirror, if she looked deeply, her eyes had a stricken, rejected look. To get rid of that she needed to be fed with conquests; regularly.

After another month or so she was laughing at dinner, making plans for more holidays, getting the bedroom curtains cleaned, and offering some of her letters from famous men for sale to American universities at very high prices. She even phoned her daughter, who sounded a bit rushed, but spoke of trying to break into the French market. Obviously Tess had no hope in that land of chic.

One day, when she didn't give a damn, he would contact her. In the safe hour. When Gogol was working on his new montage (the one made up of some bits and pieces he found in the empty flat upstairs). Of course he would. When she had no desire for him, when she had worked him out of her system.

What was it about female desire that men disliked? Was it too overwhelming? What had gone wrong with evolution? Was that why so many men these days stuck their penises up each other? When the female *animal* went into oestrus the males still responded enthusiastically. When Tess and Jack moved to Suffolk they had acquired a Labrador bitch. It went on heat early, before they had got around to getting it spayed. Every dog for miles turned up wailing and howling. They had to lock the bitch in the shed and dogs hurled themselves at it so violently one of the walls almost fell down. Finally the victor burrowed beneath the shed to mount her.

She had been on heat. She had seen her tiger eyes glowing back at her in the glass. She had growled at her reflection. A construction worker had sensed what was happening and had followed her for a few steps like a zombie. But the object of her lust had avoided her and would, until long after the spores had settled, the blast of pheromones abated; until she arrived at that exciting condition of indifference.

And it was not just because she was middle-aged (she had

been 'middle-aged' for so long, so long); even when she was young it had been the same thing. Men who had broken down her walls, burrowed under her resistance, became exhausted by her. At first they wrote poetry, concertos, books, climbed mountains, discovered new seas, then they found the prospect of endlessly servicing her debilitating. That is, if she did not have the wit to flee first; which she always did; *always*. In the past.

Only Gogol understood that she was really quite peaceful and undemanding – between bouts. Strangely, the thing Gogol adored about her was her unpredictability, and she feared that if she sat at home and knitted, like Tess, he would be profoundly disappointed in her.

One day, he phoned.

'How have you been?'

'I've been fine. How've you been?' How brisk, how unsexy her voice was. Good. 'What have you been up to' – you bastard, you pig, you mealy-mouthed incompetent, you coward?

'Oh, this and that.' He waited for her to fill the silence with her reliable sympathy.

You bastard. I'm not yielding. That was her new attitude. And she would not yield. But heard herself say, 'We're off to Prague soon. It will be strange seeing Prague again. And we'll be away for ages. *Months.*' The huffiness and the lies poured out.

'My mother has been very ill. She's in hospital. I thought she might, um . . . '

'I'm so sorry. Oh God. Is there anything I can do? No? Well, if you'd like to meet just to talk it through, certainly. Tomorrow? I'm free at tea-time.'

And so they began a series of meetings in cafés, art galleries, parks, always public places, even in restaurants,

where she often paid. He described his mother's pinched
life and obscure illnesses, or discussed Tory politics with
rage. Or censorship. They had a good old ding-dong about
censorship. She believed in censorship, always had done,
even if it meant losing a few babies with the bathwater; a
few good novels and plays. As long as the censorship was
just and intelligent. 'But who would be the censor? Who
would you trust?' he cried.

'Me. *I'd* be the censor.' Then she argued that it was
idiotic to believe for one moment that people are not
profoundly influenced by what they read and see on screens;
otherwise why would the Coca-Cola company pay so much
to promote glimpses of their can at all times? It seemed to
her that the American government was trying to solve the
population problem by training people to become serial
killers – otherwise why should there be so many films on
the subject? 'Propaganda works. Look at *Mrs Miniver* – that
film helped create the plucky attitude during the Blitz.'

'A bit before my time.'

She began to rummage in her handbag, a thing she did
when she was embarrassed.

'I'd censor the *Sun*,' he said, returning to his favourite theme: the debasement of sterling English values by
Thatcherite greed. All the Thatcherite filth would have to
go if he ruled the world.

Sometimes she was just the tiniest bit bored; not because
he was boring. She liked firebrands, always had; and his left
eyebrow still had the same knockout effect; just to be within
a yard of him caused biological havoc. But he did sound like
her first boyfriends, those communists of her youth, heckling
her for hours, for years, and all proved subsequently to be
entirely wrong.

She would sit, during these meetings, with her body angled
away from him, hardly looking at him through all her queasy

reserve. She was determined to salvage something from the fantasy. When she was away from him she tried to recollect his features. But from his face a light seemed to glow, and this light perversely obscured him. Even his coat had a lustre. Buttoned up in it, he had a dolphin shine. But she recalled with triumph that his left eyebrow went up and down when he spoke. She could cling to that through all the confusion of waning expectations.

Once she noticed he had a safety-pin on his jacket. It was then she nearly lost control, nearly told him she loved him. But she pinched her hand under the café table until the impulse faded. She was relieved at their next meeting to see that a button had been sewn on, with what looked like masculine incompetence.

Then gradually not-touching became the norm, and to remember their romantic meeting was like trying to recall a specific opera; thrilling but finite.

So they met regularly and sexlessly for months. She often became endangered by love-thoughts. There was the moment when they both waited for each other in the lobby of an art gallery (he had a lonely love of culture). She was the first to realize he must be in some other spot; she rose from her banquette and found him standing outside the revolving doors. She saw him before he saw her. She saw huge waves of loneliness around him. And she saw his gallantry and shabbiness. Quickly he rearranged his face into that sexual shine and smiled his irresistible, crooked smile. But the sadness she had seen made her long to run away with him; forget her other, deeply rooted life, fly with him towards the possibility of utter happiness on an island.

'Those girls you teach French to. They must fall in love with you. It's classic,' she said, admiring herself for the detached laughter in her voice.

'I have to be a bit careful.' Why was he such a loner? She

would never know. And he had too much sad dignity for her to probe.

Once she arrived at his place with champagne and smoked salmon and a determined expression. She opened his fridge door to look for butter, but saw only half a withered cauliflower. He sat formally behind the kitchen table. But at about one in the morning, in the middle of his diatribe about the new philistinism, she got up and left. She drove home with shaking hands. By the time she arrived there was congestion in her chest. She phoned him at two, Gogol fast asleep in another room. 'I'm finding it difficult, you know, the sexual embargo.'

He remained heavily silent. Then said, 'I've been hurt by a girl. I'm out of action in that department.'

Then, one afternoon, walking across the park, their conversation was suddenly enlivened by a lyrical mood; he kept stroking her arm, couldn't keep his hands off her; some might have interpreted it as the gestures of an affectionate child. She wanted to make love there and then under the trees with the patches of light shining off the lake all around them while they ascended into heaven. (It had been such a shambles last time, she so tense, he so brusque; she couldn't rest until she proved to him she was Venus re-created.) And it was all his fault. He had touched her again. He had created the new atmosphere.

'I wouldn't know if you were seeing another man, would I?' said Gogol that evening, enchanted to see his Aurora still a siren after all these years.

'And I wouldn't know if you were seeing another woman.' They both laughed at their ancient game.

# FIFTEEN

Gogol was pleased. It looked as if his wife was having an adventure, and for the first time he wasn't jealous. For the last few years she'd been losing her gloss, but recently, strolling through an arcade in Hampstead in which there was a stall specializing in Tess's knitwear, he had looked up and seen Aurora on the stall opposite buying dried flowers, *immortelles*, and he realized at that moment that she was also an *immortelle*.

So many of the Central European kind had popped up in Hampstead before the war, escaping the Holocaust, adding spice and intensity to British phlegm (and scholarship and skills). The English resolved their dislike of such exotica by avoiding North London, which was where these types usually chose to live, shouting to each other about impenetrable German philosophers or French nihilists, drunk on theories, blazing with ideas and gesticulating ridiculously.

Things were changing, however; old creaking houses that hadn't been renovated since they were built in the 1850s were suddenly ripped to pieces and filled with amazing numbers of bathrooms.

Dr Liebowitz, who had lived upstairs for many years, had died a few months ago, and overnight the flat was filled with the stamping boots and radio pop of builders who left copies of soft-porn magazines strewn about on the floor, all mixed up with the detritus of the Liebowitzes' life; tiny items that surviving relatives (or Oxfam) had not bothered to claim.

One night Gogol had tried the door and found it to be unlocked. He prowled around the deserted Liebowitz flat, treading on huge female bums and simpering smiles, suspenders and pubic hair. From the midst of it all he picked up the polished brass nameplate that had once been outside the Liebowitzes' apartment in Vienna, and from which they had been forced to flee one terrible endless night:

> Herr Dr L. Liebowitz
> Apartment A
> Ringstrasse 23

Gogol had stood there, breathing harshly in the empty upstairs flat, light from the street lamp and shadows from the chestnut trees pouring into the uncurtained room, and cried on the Liebowitzes' nameplate.

The next morning he resolved to sneak upstairs again and steal it; use it to create a montage of the profound poignancy of the Liebowitz syndrome. He would also steal some of the bum-and-tit pictures from the builders' magazines and work them in somewhere. Was his creative energy returning? Was he, once more, converting sorrow into the great game of art? Well, it was better than an old man crying.

When he was young he had a few years of being taken up, mainly by old pederasts, but also by buyers, and he was able to purchase a large studio in the East End to which Aurora came. That first night of her visit they became lovers. And they still were, at least in spirit. She had a little car back then (a Mini), and when she arrived on his doorstep, midnight hair atangle, siren eyes mocking and elusive, he led her upstairs into the cold, bare room and took her to bed. He had remarked on the extraordinary heat of her body, and she explained that she had rushed straight from the Ritz, where an Ethiopian prince had given her a string of rubies which she had somehow lost on the floor of her very mucky old Mini, and would he remind her to pick them up before morning.

Many decades later he persuaded her to live with him, and, as she was at one of those stages when she was a bit puzzled as to what to do next, she capitulated. He realized that he was her rod and anchor, but that to remain true to her vital nature she had to have romantic adventures.

Since she had reached a certain age, adventures were getting thin on the ground, but now, in the changed contours of her face, in the way her hair seemed to spring up in erotic anticipation and her walk had become once more as lithe as that siren with the midnight hair walking towards him over the bodies of Ethiopian princes and rubies, he read the signs of a new one. He suspected it was that dark, stocky chap who had picked her up on the cross-channel ferry months ago. He had seen, on returning from the cabin, an arc of magnetism between them; and observed with the usual wonder that she had achieved a witch-like change into a much younger woman. Travel always did that to her, of course. Plodding around Hampstead, trying to come to terms with age and realizing that going to concerts, operas, quiet dinners with cronies and occasional visits to Suffolk to see Tess and Jack were to define the limit of life's pleasures, only succeeded in reducing her to old-dried-flower status. Sometimes her lipstick was applied with too much enthusiasm and her henna was of too garish a colour for a face no longer young.

'I'll be leaving the party early, Gogol. I have to visit Arnie. He's been going through a bad time. I fear he may commit suicide,' she lied, applying make-up. She couldn't understand why Tess wore no make-up; they were all such shiny-faced puritans these days, it was as if they pointedly wanted to discourage romance. And one couldn't blame it always on AIDS. If she got AIDS well, *tant pis*, it would take ten years to kill her and she'd be dead by then anyway. Perhaps there were compensations to getting on a bit.

Gogol, listening to her plan to leave early for a rendezvous, nodded with just the right mixture of interest and indifference. Arnie, originally from Poland, was a widower of three years' standing. Gogol happened to know that Arnie was perfectly well; an Irish girl, working as his cleaner, had taken it into her head to become the mistress of this pensioner, and he was as far from thoughts of suicide as it was possible for an old man to be.

'Good idea, sweetheart. Arnie will appreciate it. We've neglected him recently.'

He approved of her first choice of dress, the cut and swathe of it; plum-coloured, but with a glow. Now she was wearing a jewelled headband, far too *jeune-fille*. And she was changing into a too tight, too short, satin skirt.

'A little overdressed,' he warned. 'It's only the Goldsteins.'

'It will cheer up Arnie.'

At the party everyone was very loud and argumentative. One of their crowd had been attacked by a roving band of young radical feminists for wearing a fur belonging to her grandmother. The fur had been the only thing she had managed to escape with on the Night of the Long Knives. When she went to the Ladies the girls had set fire to it in the restaurant and she had to be sent home in a taxi, weeping and hysterical, thinking she was back in Berlin in the thirties.

Aurora broke away from her friends and (as Gogol sweetly insisted) took his car off 'to Arnie's'. He would walk home, enjoying the stars, and she would be spared claustrophobia on the tube, lifts that suddenly broke their moorings, attackers high on crack holding knives.

It had been a wrench getting away from her friends. But now she had three clear hours to be with her lover without arousing suspicion, and in his flat too, after so many sexless meetings in cafés and museums. If patience paid off for the female spider, why not for her? But it was funny, she had never had to play patience before.

He had given her so many contradictory signals. He had not really adored her when they had that time in bed. She had sensed this, of course, and could not loosen up. Was this the same woman who had scrambled up Raoul as up a sapling as he stood, naked and shining, at a window overlooking the Via Veneto, made supple and inventive by the certainty of his love? Could that frozen stick in the council flat have been the Venus twirling on the sheets when Philippe told her he had ridden the wind?

It had been over a year since the cross-channel ferry meeting. He had wasted over a year of her precious time. Soon her breasts would sag. When that happened she would wear black and climb on the village wall.

That village wall had obsessed her ever since she saw a Fellini film in which an ageing beauty is yanked up on to it by old crones in black while she kicks and screams and insists upon the firmness of her breasts and buttocks.

Well, her breasts were still firm, thanks to breast-feeding Tatiana (Tess), who could have been sired by one of three fathers: a philosopher, a choreographer or an itinerant gypsy accordionist; and, God knows, it had been tough enough bringing up that single child. Her sulking every time they had to move to hotels; her dreariness at parties; ugly, malevolently sullen, reducing the gaiety of nations.

She should never have referred to *Mrs Miniver* and the Blitz that time with her lover – that was a close shave. He might have guessed her age.

She studied herself in the driving mirror. There was

something glittering and optimistic about the jewelled bandanna in her hair. She had taken to wearing it lately, and tonight her eyes almost matched its brightness but not quite, because when she phoned him to say she would come to his flat his voice sounded distant, wary. He did not sound amused and light like the last time they met by the lake in the park. He did not say quickly, 'Come, my flower,' but seemed to hint that he would be just as pleased to meet her in a public place and hector her about having a soft spot for Mrs Thatcher. Well, she had known worse tyrants. (But since she had heard that the BBC World Service would have to leave Bush House and set up premises in some dreary hinterland as a result of Thatcherite economic policies she no longer had the heart to defend the beast.)

Why had he sounded so dead and weary on the phone? Only two days ago they had almost made love in the park. Perhaps there was something altogether too 'planned' about the prospect of her eager arrival; perhaps she should just have turned up in all her splendid spontaneity, as she had all those years ago, driving straight from the Ritz to the East End to see that daring young painter, Gogol.

She had been a bit lonely lately. Gogol always so absorbed in his studio; the telephone so strangely silent after so many noisy years. Loneliness was an odd thing. Everyone was ashamed of it. Pathetic. The human condition. Have to be trained into it as a child. Filling the void with little distractions. Of course, she could run rings around most of the young hostesses today; but she didn't have the chutzpah to push herself forward. A good style was no use without adequate self-promotion. And, of course, flattery. Going with the fashion. Even Proust wasn't afraid to flatter and fawn; but for her it just wasn't tenable.

Aurora began the long hunt for somewhere to park that

would not be a resident's parking space or a double yellow line. The word 'Nemesis' came into her head. There was a Rue Nemesis somewhere in Paris, or had that just been a fantasy in an old movie? It was lovely to know Paris was always there, just across the Channel: the immovable feast; more reliable in its pleasure-giving than men.

When Tess lived there on her own for nearly a year back in the seventies she used to write descriptions of some favourite bar where she knitted all day. Funny how she left Paris so suddenly. And never would discuss the reason. She might as well have had a 'Keep off the Grass' sign hanging around her neck whenever one tried to probe her about it. Some tragic affair, no doubt. For she soon married that alcoholic on the rebound, which didn't last, thank God. Now she seemed to have settled for such a tame life. It seemed that 'Safety First' was her motto.

Perhaps having a child like Tess was her Nemesis. Disappointing, because she would have liked her daughter to be a soul-mate; but reassuring too that she was so solid, and with such a good business sense. Nemesis wasn't just retribution, it was just deserts.

Aurora saw an engraving once in her aunt's house in the Black Forest, of a poet at his desk in an attic, toiling by candlelight, while through the open skylight a radiant muse was descending, clothed in samite, mystic, wonderful. Nemesis would look like that. Like angels, these symbolic figures have no sex. Does this mean they are hermaphrodites or does no one ever lift their mystic, wonderful, samite?

She was still playing around with the idea of Nemesis as she reversed in front of a government building. It was a residents' parking spot, but she was prepared to risk it with Nemesis on her side. She had to believe her time had come to reap the rewards of all her unworldly devotion to pleasure and pure chance. As she struggled to leave the car she felt her skirt ride up and constrict her movements; she struggled as if in bondage. She should have worn the red dress, the one that showed off her tiny waist and breasts and cast light on her complexion. What's the use, you're past it and should have more dignity, said that tough, belittling voice, always in the background. You should think about others, stop curling your hair, you trollop, wear it in a dignified chignon.

But wives were still afraid of her, their eyes narrowing as she approached as if listening to a gale warning. She would have liked to tell them, 'You have nothing to worry about. Stealing husbands is not my style. Borrowing them, that's another story.' Their anxiety was still so funny. She sometimes looked up one of her old married lovers, popped up unexpectedly or turned up at a husband's birthday party, holding a single iris or rose, and the subsequent events became stilted, a note of hysteria entered the wife's laugh. She seldom repeated the experiment. Well, not in the same household.

She climbed the three flights, walked down the shabby corridor, pressed his bell. But the moment he opened the door she could see he was not wildly overjoyed to see her. She put her handbag between them on the sofa to prevent herself from falling into his arms. Whatever was on his mind, it wasn't erotic or amused (by life and her) as it had been in the park. It was as if the windy leaves around the lake had simply whirled off into outer darkness, leaving him even more untouchable than before.

He spent an unconscionable amount of time in the kitchen making strong tea, and the tension became unbearable. Her thwarted hopefulness. His executioner's face. This room in which she had once rolled with him on the carpet (so awkwardly) – she had to escape it. She suggested they go for a stroll, and he agreed, far too eagerly.

In the pub, after a beer or two, she found herself touching him. Strangely, sitting next to him, her hand of its own accord lifted and touched his dark hair where it sprang off his brow. But he didn't budge, didn't turn towards her, didn't melt. Didn't grin.

'What's wrong, my love?' she said very gently, worrying, worrying, worrying about the hard overhead light.

'It's my mother,' he said. 'She is ill again.'

'Oh, I'm so sorry. Is there anything I can do?'

'Well, there *is* something. But I hate to ask you, Aurora.'

'Ask away. I'll do anything.' Perhaps he wanted the name of a doctor, or to borrow money, or to find his mum a good home.

He turned his sombre eyes towards her at last, serious and dark, giving her that look. What was it about that kind of man with the bull neck and deep eyes, with sensitive, twisted mouths? She had only to see that type and her heart stopped, flew out of its closed book.

He went on sitting there, looking at her, spinning in stillness. The lights were beaming on his face, her bridegroom of the night; that meant she would still be in flattering shadow. Even if getting to him was as tough as swimming the Channel on a stormy night, she would achieve it.

'I want to ask you something important, my lovely Aurora.'

She gazed at his kind, hurt face, trembling a little, grateful for the shadows.

'Will you visit my mother? She lives in one room in Hackney and the only visitor she has, apart from me, is a cow who brings meals on wheels and bosses her around. She needs someone like you to sweep in, someone from a more *cosmopolitan* world, to visit her, to befriend her. It would make such a difference. Give her something to look forward to.' He put down his drink and said, quite cheerfully, 'After all, you would have something in common. You are about the same age.'

He said it. He said those exact words: *You are the same age.* But his mother was 80!

When he escorted her to her car, talking of this and that, she took refuge in quiet dignity. She could hardly wait to drive home, and jerked away from his goodnight peck with some violence. She had an idea that she did promise to visit his sick old mum; her *contemporary.*

She sped home, furiously gripping the wheel. In the beginning, when they were strangers, when he thought she was young, they could perform the act of love. Now she was just an old lady, like Papagena before she shed her disguise; an object of ridicule or pity. He had not thought of her 'that way' for months, not since he'd had the mirage of her, as she used to be, on the cross-channel ferry. On the other hand, yelled the mad jester, the Rude Mechanical in her head, didn't he lead you on, love (touching you up in the park)? Isn't he just another bloody neurotic with sexual hang-ups? Another bloody male?

So much ecstasy you could have had; you could both have had. But now he sees you as old, old, *old.* And 'love likes not the fruit from the withered tree.'

That night she could not sleep. Vodka had set her heart and mind raving. Gogol pretended to sleep through another of her spectacular romantic crises. He did not even remonstrate with her when he heard her in the next room frantically dialling Tess, at a time when poor Tess, exhausted from her business deals, would certainly be fast asleep.

# ALISON

## *1993*

*'We too make noises when we laugh or weep,*
*Words are for those with promises to keep.'*

W.H. Auden, *'Their Lonely Betters'*

# SIXTEEN

Grizelda is leaning over the bridge, her hair blowing in the wind from the Seine. She is facing towards the west, away from the magnetic centre. It is going to be one of those pretty pink sunsets the tourists love.

An underfed migrant walks across the bridge singing to himself. He pauses. A woman walking her dog stares at him, memorizing his long, narrow head, his dead-loser look, in case something awful happens and tomorrow she can go self-importantly to the Préfecture with his description.

All he can see of Grizelda (for her back is turned) is that hair of hers. It blazes at him, lit by the neon from a passing *bateau-mouche*, the wind separating it into strands that refract more light. A young woman alone in the evening on the Pont des Arts should not turn her back to thugs and assorted creeps for long. Unless she wants to be picked up. Unless she's dumb. Unless she doesn't give a damn. Or all three.

The drifter is struck by the hair and the smell of garlic that emanates from her. The garlic makes her seem available somehow. But there is something wrong with the street-cred clothes that mimic his poverty. He veers off, walks out of her life, for the moment, towards the shops on the other bank. He'll have to take it easy; people notice him too much. Especially if he stops too long, staring in at fancy

137

windows where the proprietors sit counting their money in their minds. All they need is one customer a week to buy some fucking great statue, like that one there. He bends down to read the card and with an effort manages it: '*The Supreme Emperor of Jade, 13th century*'. The supreme emperor of jade, just what I'm looking for, how much, keep the change. All they need is one millionaire a week; what they don't need is him hanging around the place. He isn't good for trade. When they notice him peering in at their window they give him a dirty look. How do they know he's not a millionaire? Easy. Millionaires in rags still look undeprived. It seeps out of every pore in their body; they've been valued from birth; they are all supreme emperors of jade.

He pauses in front of another shop and stares at two huge stone beasts with wings. Who'd come in and ask for these? The man who has it all, including a place for them at the end of his long gravel drive. Maybe he'd go back to that girl on the bridge and offer her a cigarette. The old trick. No, that kind of girl was more shocked if you did that than if you put your hand up her skirt.

Meanwhile Grizelda is turning around, prepared to move on. She has an unformed face, and liquorice eyes, the kind that get people into trouble. Daytime is slowly being munched up by night with bleeding gums, but you can't watch the loveliest sunset for more than a quarter of an hour, as her mother says.

Should she go back to Mum like a good girl? (Her mother is so harrowingly fussy.) A long-lost babysitter called Tess something was coming round to dinner. One of her babysitters from olden times when her mother first came to Paris, the scene of her big romance, when there was a blue dew on the world. A world she had seen in the old films that she was dragged off to for so many years: grainy black and white films with people in raincoats in the fog, and somewhere in there her mother was looking for her father. Some footage in one of the films still haunts her: a woman is turning her head among the zig-zag of shadows on a shared pillow. Why was that so curiously sexy? Why couldn't she find that feeling in life?

She strolls on through the crowds that pepper the air with their familiar French cries: *ça fait rien, m'en fous, tant pis, pas la peine, c'est la vie.* These clues to the national psyche show the attitude to be one of profound resignation. But once or twice an unresigned *dégueulasse* or *merde* rends the twilight. And, outside Samaritaine, a schoolboy on a skateboard utters the old *zut alors.*

The drifter is no longer thinking about girls on bridges or jade emperors or stone griffins, whatever they are, except he knows they must have been a 'fuck-off' sign to people like him. The song comes into his mind again: 'Sex . . . sex . . . sex', just chanted over and over like a mantra. He doesn't feel hungry any more, just strange and strung-up. Maybe he can walk it off, like walking off boredom. There is a late market up the road where white Americans shout to each other in cute corner bars. Once he put his hand through a café window, begging, and a guy placed a glass of champagne in it.

Grizelda starts walking up rue St-Denis. At the bottom, fat women stand in doorways. They resemble Breton farmworkers with their huge, shapeless flesh and wiry, wind-torn hair; the kind of arms associated with rolling pins. Men who go to them must want motherly types. (Maybe their mothers had been Breton farmworkers, in clogs and spotless white aprons.) Halfway up that street of whores the girls are all black, with long fingernails that do interesting things to orifices, and sleepy, drugged eyes.

In an alley women wait with whips, which they flick invitingly on their boots. In one doorway a girl sits with akimbo. legs, and further up a busty blonde in suspenders sways as if under sedation. Her face is powdered like an old movie star's. She leans against a window which displays the sign: '*Non-stop lesbianisme*, 100 francs.

Grizelda goes back to another bridge, the Pont Neuf. She pauses in one of the recesses to look around her at the hackneyed view: Notre Dame, the Louvre, the glittering cafés.

A black voice says, 'Gotta match, sugar?' Just like the movies. Grizelda turns around to meet tonight's Mister Midnight (that's what she calls them all). Her garlic makes him less shy. It reminds him of home in the twentieth *arrondissement* where they sleep eight to a room. It has given him ideas.

Grizelda is going to be late for her mother's dinner, as usual.

# SEVENTEEN

Tess Deutch is crossing the Luxembourg Gardens on her way to dinner in the sun-striped dusk, on her way to that same old Count's mansion. The wind blows across the surface of the ponds; the fountains blow in the changing light. She's carrying a bunch of roses. White roses seem appropriate for a reunion after such a long time. There are eighteen of them, one for each year that has slipped by so stealthily between them: Paul's wife and herself.

It's Tess's last night in Paris. Tomorrow she will be leaving, mission accomplished. And she has accomplished something in the last two days. The best young designer on the Left Bank wants her knitwear and has agreed to sell them under her 'Tessa Deutch' label. He is even prepared to sign a contract.

This morning she got the good news and, wanting to celebrate with someone, anyone, started phoning around, as if you could summon up the noisy past with a snap of your fingers. But all those drifters she had once known seemed to have evaporated. She tried not to succumb to the obvious thought, but there it was, she could always phone Alison Radcliffe. Still in the telephone book. Still in the fifth *arrondissement*. She had never given up her Paris base. Gossip columnists had kept Tess semi-informed over the years:

how Alison, the tragic widow of the brilliant diplomat, had travelled the world, even as far as New Zealand. She had eventually married again, lived in Canada with some advertising tycoon, for years. She was still gossiped about, but not with the same old avidity as after the crash. And apparently she had kept her base in Paris, the scene of the crime. Except Alison had absolutely no idea, no glimmering, that there had been any mischief involved with Paul's death. Of that Tess feels certain. Absolutely certain. The cover-up had been complete. She had thrown it away, the clue, when she threw away the letter and her life in Paris.

Tess hurries through the statues of dead queens, down the darkening steps as the gatekeeper begins to blow his whistle, minutes before closing time. The *boule* players bend to collect their balls. Only the old Japanese standing on one leg ignores the warning; continues to hold his t'ai chi position in the dusk, letting oxygen infuse his being, revelling in the present. But his leg begins to wobble.

How quickly the darkness gathers, as if hastened on by the officious whistling. The roses she carries pour out their old adorable scent; must have been plucked in the country this morning. They are not like embalmed florist's flowers. She bought them at the market on the rue de Seine, worrying about what she'd done, wanting somehow, with the roses, to propitiate her, Alison, the wife she had been blind to, the woman she had disregarded when she'd had a crush on Paul.

She slips through the shadows of Dionysus and his retinue, turns left at Chopin and right at Baudelaire. She hurries out of the gate to a storm of impatient whistles, crosses the boulevard and goes up the familiar street flanked by the Deaf and Dumb Institute wall. Outside Paul's house she stops, feeling queasy, feeling like a double agent. But the top strand of her wants company, talk and warmth. Wants to live on the surface.

She could have got company in the café she just walked by, where an impromptu band was warming up with be-bop. She could have drunk Pernod after Pernod in honour of her younger self, watching the tourists and vagabonds: *cette parade sauvage*. Coming here was probing a sore place, making things worse, peering into Pandora's box. This city! Rimbaud got it right. He saw through it with his blue-white laser eyes: '*Paris the whore. Although it is frightful to see you again . . . your Beauty is Marvellous.*' Was it all thanks to the architecture of Haussmann? Or the position of the city, wrapped around the river? With its islands like clitorises? It was definitely feminine gender. And as full of sin and ugliness as Gomorrah.

For years she avoided the place. But sometimes, late at night, lying in bed in London or New York (both cities in which she had established outlets), her power-suit hanging on the hotel trouser-press, unable to sleep, she'd recite herself to sleep at last with Métro stops: *St Sulpice – St Germain des Prés – Odéon – St Michel – Châtelet – Les Halles – Réaumur-Sébastopol – Strasbourg-St-Denis*. The train thundered on into the dark.

In a dream, a tramp at Odéon Métro erected a table with a wobbly leg. He produced a napkin, put it on the table (which rocked dangerously), uncorked a bottle of champagne and toasted Tess as she stared at him from her dream train on the opposite platform. Such gaiety in misfortune. Such *finesse*.

She pushes apart the double doors, still painted that deep French green, but flaking here and there, and enters the lost domain. Her footsteps echo up to all the windows in all the flats as far up as the *chambres de bonnes* under the grey mansard roof. What were eighteen years but a blink of the eyelid in the centuries since this house was built? But some things have changed, the word over the lodge is no longer *concierge* but *gardienne*.

The gravel slides noisily at her feet, warning them all of

the approach of a time-monster. She begins the climb to the flat. The parquet squeaks, the banisters shine, the late dusk flattens itself against the window. Opposite, a willow dangles over the Deaf and Dumb garden wall, fronds waving. That willow was much smaller when she broke into this flat that chilly dawn. Her hands are shaking now as they were then.

Foolish to have come back. Had she felt she could pretend it hadn't happened, just sail along on the surface, like when she bumps into her ex-husband? They smile, they joke, and there is anaesthesia between them, for if there weren't they would run at each other with a hatchet.

She had married someone out of panic (and vanity) after Paul died. That juvenile marriage had been an error, but he had been her intimate friend (for a while), and now when they run into each other all she sees is just another punter who keeps bobbing up against the odds. Sometimes she wishes she could strike out at him: tie him to a chair, list her grievances – with colour slides. It might reduce the numbness. But perhaps the numbness is a legacy from Paul.

And here she is about to smile right into his wife's face. Get through an entire evening without spilling the beans. Keeping secrets is honourable work, but usually unrewarded, except in a smug sense of one's own moral strength.

She puts her hand on the knocker. Will Grizelda be there? Will there be a table laid for three with fine napery and china (very fine, because Alison is rich; rolling in it, lucky woman).

She knocks. She hears footsteps approach, the bark of an idiot dog. She hates dogs like that, silly yappy dogs that old ladies brush and comb; doubtless it will fart and scratch, but it might be a useful tool for diverting conversation away from any precipices.

The door is opened cautiously by an unfamiliar woman who is crouched down holding on to the collar of the crazed animal.

'Tess, how lovely,' she gasps.

Tess follows her in and, while Alison issues futile commands to the dog, goes on ahead into the *salon*, glancing with sick eyes at the mantelpiece. There it is. The eighteenth-century clock with its bust of winged whoever in front of which a letter had once been propped that could have been full of Semtex for the damage it would do; the letter she took and threw into the Seine, somewhat dramatically. It drowned so slowly.

She turned away from the loaded mantelpiece. Alison is edging back into the room, flushed, different, much softer-looking than when she was married to Paul.

'Terriers. Grand little watch-dogs. Oh, what lovely roses. Tess, you look great. A little severe, a little,' she laughs, 'like an avenging angel.'

Tess sits down, tries to relax, consciously lowers her shoulders, amazed at how high and tense they had been.

'The flat is bigger than I remember.' The mad dog comes and sits next to her. She cautiously pats him, although she loathes terriers. (She's a Labrador person.) Perhaps he isn't so bad. None of us can help our reflexes. Our mad collection of ancestors.

'I remember you used to always drink Pernod, Tess.'

'I thought it was sophisticated. I'll have whisky now though, if you've got it.'

Got it? Of course she's got it. You could tell by the vastness of choice in her cabinet that she was no alcoholic. Tess's ex-husband had been an alcoholic, and there would never at any moment have been any undrunk drink in his house.

She would not have recognized Alison if she'd sat opposite her on the Métro. Perhaps she had never really noticed her before. As she moves about, setting up the drinks, she reveals a stately body clothed in St Laurent casuals. What fills Tess with ease, despite the heavy sub-text, is Alison's complete lack of self-consciousness; how catching that is. Had money given her this new calm? Had she been properly loved somewhere along the line? What had happened to the receding chin? Had it just been part of her large, rather unattractive repertoire of displacement activities – holding in her chin to ward off blows? Now she had quite a normal chin, although there was the beginning of a second one beneath it, and her hands and hair had the cruel stamp of age.

At 36, Tess is still on the long plateau between youth and age; only faintly aware of the long shadows approaching.

'You're a success! I read about your knitwear in the *Trib.*'

'How's Grizelda? What's she up to?'

Alison puts down her gin and stares at the glass. 'Out wandering the streets as usual. Goes out almost every night. Sometimes never comes back until dawn. And then she looks a wreck, as if she's been splattered up a wall somewhere. But tonight she's promised she'll come back. She wants to meet you, Tess. Anyone who knew her father she loves to meet. She'll want to know every little detail you can dredge up.'

Tess starts, hoping she won't come back, hoping she'll stay safely splattered up some wall somewhere.

'She was a lovely child, but at adolescence she began to torment me. She knows I hate the smell of garlic, but she eats a whole head of garlic every day. It's bizarre.'

'I heard of a boy who ate the heads off frogs; much worse.'

'She's not that bad. But still . . . *garlic.* The one thing I hate.'

'That's the point, surely.' Tess gulps whisky without tasting the stuff. Alison is still hopelessly English. To dislike garlic is to dislike life. The terrier is on her lap and she is stroking the brute out of nerves. 'I'm glad you never gave up this place.'

'In your day it was twelve hundred francs a month. Now

it's a million.' They laugh at each other. Paul is laughing back at Tess. He is in her eye-line, a young Ganymede standing in the quad, his blazer over one shoulder, his smouldering looks tamed and modified by English repression, an apparent self-deprecation. His photograph is on the piano in a silver frame. Solid silver, of course, this being the maisonette of the widow who collected that huge insurance. But she had gained after his death in more ways than that. She changed personalities; acquired stature when she adopted the widow's weeds.

'You married again, didn't you, Alison?'

Alison shrugs, gives a rueful smile. Divorce is not quite as funny as inflation. They both bury their heads in their drinks. Tess waits, rolling the whisky around in her glass, counting the rolls: one, two, three, four. It is a little trick she learned in her youth, a trick for sweating out a pregnant silence. It had been enormously productive during some of her business meetings.

'There was a Canadian. Nice. But.' She gives a mirthless chuckle. 'Ran off with his secretary.'

'Did he sock you for a lot of money?'

'He was *nice*. I told you. But what could he do, poor man? After seven years with me, he fell in love with pert little Miss Smith – *boing*.'

'Boing, boing.' They laugh again. 'Seven years isn't bad, Alison. It's about as long as I've had with Jack. But perhaps he is experiencing the "boing" right at this moment back in Suffolk where we live now.' Tess gives a fake shudder. She knows she can rely on her Jack.

Alison looks at her with caution. Perhaps she expects an avalanche of confessions: two women together after such a long stretch; time for the letting down of hair, the display of wounds, the demand for maternal comfort. She doesn't have to worry, Tess is not going to confess a tragic love affair, she's never had such a thing, nor is she going to unwind the banal story of her marriage to the alcoholic. She and Jack, her business partner, have vowed to stick by each other to the end. But they have never bothered to make it legal. Why torment the gods with ceremonial optimism? It was different when women were breeding machines, when babies popped out each spring like blossom. Time was too brief for exploring each other's depths, let alone the shallows where the rocks that most marriages flounder on tend to be. Her great-grandmother had ten children. She had no time for luxuries like divorce; like romance.

Jack and she agree that the 'boing' kind of love is for the birds. Look what it had done to her old mother. Made mincemeat of her every time. She is getting (and Tess hates to see it) quite pathetic. After every adventure she looks more mangled, more self-doubting. And self-doubt is bad for those legendary looks of hers. At least Gogol is there in the background. He fell for her in her youth and never wavered; never sees her as 'old', it seems. Mother doesn't realize his value. She only notices his growing seediness, without realizing that she shares the condition.

In Alison's *salon* not a yard of wall is without an original painting in the sub-impressionist style – all pleasant enough, but without the authority of the giants of that school who painted the world the way it looks when you're happy. The way it looked when Tess's first husband courted her; running up the stairs, his arms full of flowers, making her laugh. She laughed all the way to the registry office. She thought he drank just like everyone drank. But he was a Dr Jekyll and Mr Hyde drinker. And when Dr Jekyll woke in the morning in a room full of metaphorical blood he became irritated if his attention was called to any of Mr Hyde's misdemeanours. So she was left choking on outrage.

'Some of your paintings remind me of the things Gogol used to do.'

'Gogol?'

'Mother's current lover.'

'People who grow old with style give the rest of us hope, don't they?'

Tess says nothing to that, but starts to praise one of the pictures. Alison tells her what artists she encourages, what galleries she supports. There are some compensations to having everything money can buy.

Tess is not doing so badly herself. The knitwear business took off when she devised a way of incorporating Monet's water-lilies and Van Gogh's sunflowers into her patterns. By now she's brought things to a point where she uses less obvious emblems (hence the interest from the French boutiques). At present she is working out a way of knitting a de Kooning with a very fine weave. She's been toiling over graphs all afternoon in her hotel. Her eyes are still sore from the exertion. She will soon need glasses.

Alison stands up. 'Let me take you on the tour before dinner. But not much has changed, you'll see.'

The obedient guest follows her out of the room, lets the terrier slide to the parquet. Shutting the door behind her, she glances back at Paul: so young; so dead.

They walk up the inner staircase through poster after poster of old movie stars: Jean Gabin, Michèle Morgan in her wet mac, Arletty, Louise Brooks, Humphrey Bogart staring moodily through cigarette smoke, his coat collar up. This is a new aspect of Alison. Or had it been there all the time, even when she was a crushed housewife, this *nostalgie* for *film-noir* romance? Of course, Tess had hardly noticed her at that crucial time. She had noticed Paul with too close and lethal attention to have given a moment of real observation to his wife; reflexive politeness, of course, as they dealt with questions of gripe water, the nappies, or the jumpers she knitted as she waited for Mr and Mrs Radcliffe to return, Paul deliciously surly, his wife tense and clumsy.

On the landing the posters are all of French writers: Rimbaud with undone cravat; Colette, kohl-eyed and shrewd, a foppish Proust, Malraux, cigarette stuck on lower lip. And Camus exuding intelligence and sexiness in equal measure, a face like Paul's only tougher. The face he might have grown into.

Alison opens the door to his old study and they enter the huge room. Tess stands, stock-still, as if she has just had a vision of him sitting over there in his swing chair, at his long teak desk.

Nothing has been changed. Alison has changed nothing, like Miss Havisham. Except, unlike the old lady's bridal-decked chamber, there is no dust, no grime, no cobwebs, no sense of stale loopiness. Things are even tidier than ever, that's all, as neat as in all museums of the dead.

His famous black coat is draped over the chair where (Alison believes) he last draped it, its astrakhan collar still glossy, still signalling that its owner is/was a man of sub-stance. On his long desk the Schaeffer fountain pen with his engraved initials is parallel with the silver Schaeffer pencil. His ink well, the old brass demon-head, is filled with black ink. (Alison must top it up when it dries out in the central heating.) His papers are piled on the cabinet in meticulous order. Tess looks at the bookcase, recognizing *The Romantic Agony*, *The Screwtape Letters*, *The Golden Bowl* and *Hard Times*.

Two oars from his rowing triumphs are still on the wall with the photograph of Paul in the winning team. His squash racket rests in the corner as alert as if he'd just swung into the room with it; its strings taut and ready for a match in the Luxembourg Gardens in which even English gentlemen can express their murderous competitiveness without drawing blood. And there is the photograph of him lined up with the school squash team at the age of 16.

She turns and stares at the spare bed. Paul had transported it all the way from his mother's house in Sussex. How the workmen had huffed and puffed carrying it up the winding stairs. She is surprised not to find a rope stretched in front of it to prevent museum visitors from soiling the cover.

Tess is hugging herself like someone coatless in Siberia. 'I remember the coat,' she murmurs. 'The astrakhan lapels. A bit flashy for Paul.'

Alison is watching her; she must be careful. The widow has acquired a quiet majesty in her shrine. She stands quite calmly, and for the first time her friendly face is still and Tess can see her eyes clearly. In repose she looks as if she has only just stopped crying. Is that a permanent look? Did it drive away the jolly Canadian, defeated by her eternal widow's weeds; the priestess of sorrow, the keeper-of-the-flame?

The noise of the ice clinking in her glass reminds her there is succour to hand. She drinks the lot in one gulp, standing there, feeling claustrophobia mounting slowly as it does in a very slow and creaking lift.

'Of course, I kept this room locked when we lived in Canada. The tenants did not have a key.' Alison leads her back across the landing to her old bedroom, which is completely redecorated and ghost-free. Then they move to Grizelda's room, which looks unused, more unused than Paul's study, as if, somehow, she is more dead than he, more truly absent.

'Can't you just buy it outright, this flat? Stop forking out the colossal rent?'

'The Count won't sell any of the apartments. This house has been in his family since it was built. He'll hold on to it for ever.'

They are on their way downstairs. The movie stars blur

151

their way past Tess's eyes, their mixture of style, mystery and sex appeal still potent after all these years, leaving her icy cold.

Downstairs she notices this time that the dining table is set for three. Grizelda will turn up at any moment. She needs another drink. A gust of night wind pushes open the french windows and they can hear the flapping of the willow against the Deaf and Dumb wall. A night of warm wind like this could bring the spring in one morning. But sometimes the heavy cold rains beat it back.

Over the next drink Alison tells her ex-babysitter about how she first left England, how she wangled a job as secretary at the British Council in Warsaw; how she had been born – the second child – to very old parents who ran an Edwardian hotel on the front at Eastbourne. They had been deeply upset by their son, who liked to hurt small animals. She showed Tess a snapshot of the hotel and of herself as a 10-year-old, a squinting nonentity standing on a circular drive in front of a flower clock.

Meeting Paul in Poland, she had found glamour. Flowers were no longer clocks.

'But what about you, Tess? Have you been with Jack for a long time?'

'Years. Before that I was married, for a few bizarre months, to an alcoholic. One day, do you know what he did? He unravelled an entire coat I had been hand-knitting for three months. He really wanted to unravel *me*. But he couldn't, I was ploddingly indestructible, like Mama.'

'Have another drink. Now you're not living with an alcoholic you can drink as much as you like without setting a bad example.'

'Well, on an empty stomach . . . '

'Grizelda hasn't kept her promise. We might as well start without her.'

Tess makes no effort to spring up and assist, but sits there, still hypocritically stroking the dog, letting Alison bustle about in the tiny adjacent kitchen. She gazes with an archaeologist's eye at the walls. How many layers of paint have there been since she took the letter? Can walls see? Remember? Does the sediment of fear bury itself in the masonry and affect the atmosphere? This ancient house must have witnessed worse crimes in the revolution: the haulings-off in the night, the echoes of tumbrils. The walls are stiff with the past, an assemblage of ghosts, including her own ghost mouthing Paul's name, lips distorted, puzzled by the curious effrontery of time. She is just one of the great ghost army. It is her heavy tread Alison hears at night, moving about back and forth, back and forth in the small hours, across the parquet. Always the same route, from the door to the mantelpiece, stopping dead by the clock.

'I hope you like meat?' Alison puts down the *gigot* on its pretty plate. 'You're not one of those vegetarians that proliferate around the globe?'

'I'm an unreconstructed carnivore.'

'I thought I smelt blood.'

Tess pushes away the terrier, who shakes himself, yawns, and slinks off to his basket. But Alison is smiling. When she smiles you can't see her wept-dry eyes. They shrink to merry slits.

Why does she feel guilty? All she did was try to spare Alison unending unnecessary pain. But she does feel guilty. She'd gone over and over it. She should have seduced Paul, that night, after he had dumped all that on her, she should have asked him up to her room, been the Cossack's plaything; perhaps it would have siphoned off his frustration. Or maybe she should have begged him not to go to the airport; thrown herself under the taxi, refused to deliver the letter. Made him think again, think about Grizelda.

153

'It would be no hardship to be a vegetarian these days – meat tastes so awful.'

'This is French. The lambs run about on hillsides and dance jigs.'

'I see, they express themselves fully. Learn the violin. Attend opera. Go to encounter groups . . . '

Flowers cast shadows on glass, crystal and porcelain. The table gleams, as Tess predicted, with silver on damask, but above Grizelda's chair absence weighs. A hole has been cut out of the air.

'So tell me about Jack.'

'Solid as a rock. My anchor.'

'I wouldn't have thought you needed an anchor, Tess. You're rather like an anchor yourself.'

'Hmmm . . . ' She cuts the lamb, tender and pink inside. 'Two anchors anchored together, but where's the bloody ship?'

'Paul used to say – that girl, she'll do for us. Solid as a rock. The reliable kind. You can see it in her face.' (And he used to add 'and her disapproving mouth', but of course Alison doesn't pass on that piece of pain.)

'I'm not sure that's very flattering.'

'And knitting all the time. Nobody knits. At least, they'd stopped back then. Maybe you started the fashion for fancy knits. I always used to stop halfway through. Got bored. Gave up. You were an anachronism. Plugged on until you cast off.' She passes the mint sauce. It was ridiculous to be served mint sauce in Paris. 'So, business is good, then? All that dogged patience rewarded?'

'Fine. Fine. But I want to hear more about Grizelda. How is she really?'

Alison passes her the dish of broccoli although she has already served herself. There is a silence, the bronze clock ticks. 'She was a lovely child.'

154

'I remember.'

'No, I mean up until she was about twelve. Lovely. And . . . watchful . . . noticed things other people didn't. A bit disconcerting – always turning over stones to see what crawled beneath. Not popular at school. Always brought home the hopeless ones.' Alison was staring at the hole above the empty chair. Chantal with huge, tormented eyes whose mother insisted on burdening her, aged 10, with all the horrors of the concentration camps, in detail. Alison thought she had become a prostitute of sorts. And then Pascale, who lived with her parents in a *chambre de bonne* the size of a loo and seemed to squash herself small, not only physically but mentally, in order to take up as little room in the world as possible.

'Empathy! A lovely characteristic in a child. Even when it is plain old pity.'

'That was at the Ecole des Filles. In Toronto it got worse. Maybe she didn't like my having another man. But you know it was bad for her to think she had a sexless, lonely eunuch as a mother. He, that is, Clem, he was a lovely big bear of a chap. You'd think she'd have warmed to him; responded. God knows he tried. Tried with both of us.'

'So then what?'

'Ah . . . ' Alison downs her glass without savouring her precious 1969 Latour. 'The waifs and strays she brought home just got worse. Even a bit scary. They stole, of course.'

'Was she clever at school?'

'Amazingly. At first. A bit of a prodigy. Then, well, she just stopped trying when she hit adolescence. Started to goad me. Like with the garlic-chewing.'

'Maybe sex took over. The roar of the hormones.'

'How I wish it were as simple as that. How I wish there

had been a series of gauche boyfriends. But let's change the subject. Have some *tarte Tatin.*'

'Did you make it?'

'That would be foolish in Paris. This is their art form. Tell me, Tess, how do you think up those marvellous ideas for your designs? Who would have thought my babysitter would become a famous designer . . . '

'Hardly . . . ' So they discuss her business, then her undemanding lover, Jack and move back to less trouble-some waters. How lovely the room is, so much warmer in atmosphere than it used to be, if a little too cluttered.

She had been getting morbid back there, with that ghost fantasy. Not seeing the present for the past; belaboured by the bloody past as usual.

# EIGHTEEN

The dog lets out an irresolute whimper from the depths of a dark dog dream. It is eleven-thirty and Grizelda has neither shown up nor phoned. Alison needs to be entertained, needs to be distracted from the thought of her daughter wandering in the night.

*(Night after night Alison lies awake, trying to read, glasses slipping down her Niveaed nose, wondering where her daughter is, out there somewhere in the chomping jaws of the city. And even if she manages to fall asleep she dreams of Grizelda. Grizelda in some hole; in dread; an irresolute shadow on some grimy wall. The predator, his face masked, moves closer, closer . . . )*

She rummages on the floor for her cigarettes, extracting one from the packet with her teeth, then slumps back again on the yellow sofa, holding the light dangerously close to her eyelashes; getting the angle wrong. She doesn't want to let Tess go; any excuse to take her mind off Grizelda. *(Grizelda in the morgue, Grizelda being raped in a parking lot. Grizelda locked in the boot of a car. Grizelda lost on the darkling plain outside the cosily lit, well-furnished room where privileged women sprawl, gossiping.)*

She had been telling Tess about how it all started with Paul. Soon after they met they went to a poetry reading organized by the British Council in Warsaw. Later he admitted that he preferred the classics and recited her the last lines from 'Dover Beach':

Ah, love, let us be true
To one another! for the world, which seems
To lie before us like a land of dreams,
So various, so beautiful, so new,
Hath really neither joy, nor love, nor light,
Nor certitude, nor peace, nor help for pain;
And we are here as on a darkling plain
Swept with confused alarms of struggle and flight,
Where ignorant armies clash by night.

Alison knew then that he needed her. She was Dover Beach; she was England, home and mother. Was that the night she conceived Grizelda, the night of the darkling plain? She believed it was.

To die not having given birth will probably be Tess's fate. Tess wonders if she is a coward. Or perhaps the world appals her too much to participate in it with more gumption than is absolutely necessary.

It is past midnight. Through the window a few meagre stars shine above the Deaf and Dumb Institute, and in one of the rooms in the corner hotel lights are still blazing. But most of Paris is tucked up for the night, including the Count in the flat next door dreaming of the days when his ancestors were the sole occupants of this city château. They could no longer hear the crowd pulsing down the boulevard. At its height it seems no more nor less crowded than it used to be, but the traffic is worse and the beggars more aggressive. There are more blacks, but fewer sad Algerians who used to hang about on the edges of pavements like curs, and just as despised. They are now running small businesses in the *banlieue* where streets pulse with migrants of all colours who possess strength through numbers.

Even here in the bourgeois zone, Arab graffiti are scrawled on every naked smooth surface; signs of solidarity or threats. When Tess was on the Métro yesterday, on her way from the Opéra, a gypsy beggar child wailed flamenco for four stops. Even when the train jerked to a halt, pushing some of the standing passengers to the ground, the girl didn't pause for a single beat, oblivious of the vagaries of fate, as befitted her Romany blood. When the train started up again Tess grimaced with relief at the African mother nursing her baby opposite. The woman stared back with inexplicable venom at Tess in her discreet shades of beige, clutching her huge shoulderbag like a vice, advertising the fact that there was money in it.

'So, Tess, how's your mother?'

Tess wonders if she ought to leave, ring for a taxi. But something holds her back. She does not feel she has overstayed her welcome. Every time a silence descends Alison hooks her with another question. Now it is time for her mother to make an entrance. Time for comic relief.

'Through all her troubles, Mother remained completely confident that rescue was to hand; and you know, Alison, it always was. But I was worried. Here come the days of an old rouged courtesan taking meals on wheels, I thought, and then Gogol galloped in like the Canadian Mounted Police.'

'He's quite a good painter, isn't he?'

'He had a reputation once, and then he got stalled somehow in mid-career, probably some trauma or something took away his confidence and he only made hopeless, hopeless messes whenever he put brush to canvas. But he has family money, thank God. And he's *nice*. Mum has enough sense to stick to him. So that's all right. They potter around their flat in Belsize Park not noticing the dust.'

'Not seeing it, perhaps?'

'Mother won't wear glasses, of course. Too vain. The only time she ever went to an optician she had the misfortune to get a very handsome one, so of course she was obliged to lie about her age.'

'But naturally.'

'He was so thrilled to find a patient with a previous record of twenty-twenty vision who had developed the long sight of people a decade older that he wrote jubilantly off to report his finding to the *Lancet*.'

'I've been right, all my life, never to trust statistics, so often based on lies of that sort,' laughs Alison.

She has always had a surprisingly nice laugh; at least, surprising when she was that other Alison: skin drawn too tight over her cheeks; anxious eyes, hen-like movements that made one want to slap her to a standstill. But now, look, she is the kind of woman Paul might have loved: soft, swarming, warm, even a bit messy. She has lost that deadly killjoy neatness, that reflex to wash up before dinner ends, to ruin an atmosphere fussing over something spilled. Paul was like that at his worst, and when the two of them were at it things became impossibly brittle: flowers withered, sauces refused to thicken, babies never stopped crying.

When Tess goes upstairs, rising through the display of smouldering movie stars, she sees that Alison has left the key in Paul's shrine. She cannot resist it, but on leaving the lavatory she opens the door and enters the forbidden zone, tiptoeing across the silence, pushing through the sepulchral light. She stands there and caresses the astrakhan coat collar. She had been too timid to touch Paul when she had the chance. Too scared and proud, when he hovered at the door of her hotel.

She picked up the old broken brolly they carried about that long night of confessions, that *nuit blanche* when he put too much responsibility on her shoulders, responsibility that got heavier with the years, the silent crush of it afflicting her like gravity.

She conceals the umbrella in one of the many yellowing copies of the *New York Herald Tribune* piled on his desk. She takes it downstairs to the entrance and smuggles it among her coat and bag. The movie stars smoulder their eyes down at her. The keepers of the flame, any flame, false flames notwithstanding.

She plans to throw the broken umbrella in a bin in the Luxembourg Gardens, as if she could rewind the film; do something which would symbolize far more than getting rid of an old brolly. Some things should be thrown out, forgotten. Otherwise the world gets too cluttered. One can't breathe if the past becomes stronger than the present.

Back in the *salon* Alison is lying there on the sofa, blank-eyed, staring at nothing. Just lying there like Niobe, all tears. But she is all cried out, no actual tears drip. How could there be any left after eighteen years of it?

Tess wonders if she can gather courage. Take a deep breath. Speak out. Rescue her from her sorrow. Spit it out. Tell her she is grieving, has been grieving all these years for nothing, sweet fuck all; deliver the *coup de grâce*.

# NINETEEN

The clock pings three times. It is their darkest hour. The hostess has been dozing on the sofa; the dog snoring in its basket, beset by dreams of struggle and flight. Tess cannot decide whether to tiptoe out of the flat, leave a note, thank you and goodnight. Alison, one arm dangling on parquet (cramp will wake her soon), is breathing harshly like an old and sorrowful horse. She needs to have her mane stroked, be comforted with apples.

Hers is not an enviable situation, despite wealth. Her daughter, the vampire. As the sun falls Grizelda leaves the house, returning the next morning with a sullen-accusing look on her face, something the hell-cat dragged in.

This is sapping her mother, disabling her more completely than Paul's death, but is also a consequence of it. (But this vampire, contrary to tradition, carries her own garlic, which might protect her from herself.)

Alison jerks up, blinks, rubs her forearm. Tess stands looking out into the dark garden. Behind her she hears a series of yawns, heavy footsteps thudding out of the room.

On the shadowy wall opposite it is just possible to see the old white imprinted words: '*La loi de*' something, followed by a date, '*187-*'. Paul once told her it was a law forbidding post-revolutionaries to write on walls. A shadow seeps along the length of its cobbled surface, attached to a strolling policeman. Even his shadow conveys loneliness, boredom. A boy from the country who joined the police force because it offered adventure. He bangs his baton against the stones: thud, thud, thud. He stops next to the *clochard* sleeping on the air vent and plucks a paperback from his limp hands. He flicks through a few pages, standing there, a wistful figure under the street light.

'Isn't it time we called the police?'

'Police! They'd laugh at me. I'm the local nuisance. I've called them out once too often to scour the city. Or they'd threaten to take her up before a magistrate this time.'

'Charged with what?' Tess joins her in the kitchen as she makes another pot of coffee.

'Oh, they'd think of something.' Alison yawns. Her guest leans against the door jamb watching her; Grizelda is punishing Alison and plucking out her own feathers in the same vindictive process.

At the memorial service in London Alison had glowed like a bride. She did not resort to the melodrama of a Jackie Kennedy veil, but she did wear black from head to foot. Tess was struck by how much taller she looked, how much better her posture, the tilt of her head. She no longer had that loser's crouch that invites rebuke.

Tess arrived late at the service and stood to one side in her new Biba raincoat, with the collar up. Somewhere among all those hundreds of people (Paul had never been a marginal figure) must be Tom and Beth Scrutton (that is, if Beth wasn't in hospital somewhere, under sedation). But there were so many middle-aged women, and none marked with high tragedy, other than Alison, the star of the occasion.

Anyway, it was unlikely that the Scruttons and she could recognize each other and she, at least, made no serious effort

164

to do so, but decided to slip away before the end to avoid the possibility of confrontation.

Just inside the church door (with the other late arrivals) a family stood, staring at her, as if they knew her intimately. They had to move aside if she was going to leave. The man slowly took off his glasses. He mouthed his name in her ear in a whisper: *Tom Scrutton. You're Tess, aren't you?* The woman with him must be her; *Beth.* She was surrounded by beautiful young people; must be her children. Two young men on one side; a young woman on the other; all supporting her, physically, morally; all with the same Welsh eyes, the same springy hair. Beth was clutching a handkerchief, her cheeks blotched with mascara, but she kept giving her brood a series of quick little smiles as if to reassure them that she would be all right; she would not die of grief; life was longer and inexpressibly richer than trauma and loss.

That woman had everything, *everything.* Tess could not control it: the sword of jealousy.

She shoved past without reacting to Tom and hurried out, down the steps and away down a miserable London street. When she heard footsteps following her she turned and said. 'Mr Scrutton, I'm sorry, I . . . '

'That's all right.' Tom took her arm. How like a journalist: overweight, showing signs of drink, but with shrewd, shrewd eyes.

They walked on a bit. It was like pushing through sheets of metal.

'I think Paul would have been amused by that crowd, don't you?'

'Would he?'

Tom looked at her quizzically. He knew Paul's social orbit. She did not. She was simply a sort of servant. She looked back and saw Beth and her bulwark of children standing on the church steps, watching them.

'Do you still live in Paris, Tess?'

'I'm back here now. Starting a business; selling my own knitwear. Sick of Paris.'

'Thank you for what you did. It worked. No bones broken.'

'No.' No bones broken. No hearts broken. She was not sure about that. It seemed to her there had been every conceivable kind of breakage. But she couldn't say a word, couldn't think of a word to say.

Tom went on standing there; did he want to be congratulated on his cover-up job? Why was he so pleased with himself? Maybe because he had his beautiful wife back and she would have to be grateful for ever; after all, he had averted a greater tragedy; even more mess.

'Goodbye, then.'

'Goodbye.'

'And I don't need to tell you – ' He held his finger to his lips and mimed a theatrical 'ssshhh'.

She watched him walking back to join his family. In the distance Beth held up her hand to Tess in a curious, cramped wave. It felt like a mixture of acknowledgement and exoneration, or perhaps thanks.

Tess walked away from them all, fists dug in her pocket, sorry she hadn't been able to hold on to Tom for a little longer. Talking to him might have helped clear her mind, clear the debris. After all, he and she were conspirators. They were the only ones who knew the real story (story?), apart of course from Beth, and now the children. Since the crash, whenever she had tried to think of Beth she could only see her waiting in some hotel in Marseilles, quivering with joy and longing, about to sail off to Casablanca, like in the old movies. After that everything dissolved. But Beth was over there, standing on the steps, blowing her nose, surrounded by her offspring. Beth was surviving. Would survive.

Tess hurried away from them all. Then, in that miserable London street, she felt a small metallic object under the lining of her raincoat. She drew it out, the key to the Paris flat of Paul and Alison. It scalded her hand. She threw it into the gutter where it rolled through a grid into the sewers below London to join the bones of the dinosaurs.

Tess had told Tom Scrutton she was sick of Paris, but here she is in Paris again and not sick of it at all. Some things had got worse, some better, under the law of flux. The great paintings have changed galleries; if looking could wear things out they would all have evaporated by now. Streets, tarted up in the eighties by developers (almost killed off as far as the charm of centuries was concerned), had recently rumbled back to life in the hardy form of small-traders: feather dusters, metal ladders, ironing boards and vegetables cluttered the pavements. After all, someone has to service the rich. Feather dusters outside shops are not what the developers had in mind, but they can't control it, just as they can't control the leaves.

This morning she stopped to buy a poster from a river bookstall. It was a copy of the Declaration of the Rights of Man.

'Ah, you like it, madame?' (When would they have stopped calling her mademoiselle?) 'But none of us can live up to it,' joked the bookseller.

'We're no angels,' she countered.

'Can't live with an angel.'

'Worse perhaps with a devil.'

They were dancing the ancient minuet of flirtation.

He took a swig from his thermos. 'Ah, it is terrible this collapse of the Left. This disillusion.' He snapped elastic around the poster. 'It would have been better for us old communists if we had remained Catholics.' And he grinned.

He was part of the culture that could never happen again if a million monkeys copulated on a million planets in every known temperature. When she left him she walked through a bizarre manifestation of antique dealers who strolled down the rue du Bac, expensive clothes billowing, and all with the co-operation of the *flics*, snarling up traffic even further.

But now this heavy night she is not skidding on the droll surface, scooping off the cream that is always accumulating in Paris, waiting for everyone's next visit. Paris might be a better place for visitors than for those who live here. A better lover than spouse. Out there now it's got Grizelda in its jaws.

'Why is Grizelda like this? Why does she do this to herself?'

Alison carries the tray into the room; Tess follows her. She sits down, and everything in her body flops. She gazes ahead wearily and Tess regrets her question. 'Grizelda drank in loss and sorrow with her mother's milk.'

Tess sips coffee. She will get coffee jitters. But she can't stop, or leave. Alison may be dying for her to leave, praying for it, but she can't smell it on her. She wants diversion, doesn't want another rotten all-night vigil on her own, waiting for the bad news, the visit to the morgue.

Grizelda drank in sorrow and loss with her mother's milk. After the post-shock elation which Tess saw at the memorial service there would have been the relentless thudding of blind loss. Loss of something perfect. Perfection lost leaves the worst wounds. It can never return; it's against the law of averages.

And so for Grizelda it must have been loss for break-fast, dinner and tea. Alison bending over her in her cot, emanating waves of loss; sitting alone after guests had gone, twiddling a spoon, *loss*; welcoming her back from school, *loss*. And when they tried living in hearty Canada, even watching cheer-leaders twirling their pom-poms: *loss, loss, loss.*

Photographs of her father (the perfect specimen) were as remote as the faces of Bogart, Gabin, Gérard Philipe, that gazed down on hers from their shining posters high in the firmament of the past.

'I suppose I've been mourning Paul all of her conscious life,' Alison says. 'Still am, I suppose. I thought I'd escape it in Canada among all that wheat. But that was a pretence. A sincere pretence. I've tried to hide it, be brave, but all the time I was destroying Grizelda. The present to her seemed cheap.'

Now she begins to cry. Not dry sobs but the overflowing of a brimming dam. And Tess had thought she was all cried out.

Tess picks up things from the floor (cup, saucer, cigarettes and the peelings of an orange eaten absent-mindedly at an earlier hour). Yes, she's found another water-table below the widow's grief, ranker water containing maternal guilt.

'Do you want a tissue, Alison?'

She doesn't reply, but stares weeping into the middle-distance where ghosts live, and chimeras. Tess feels dirty, and very exhausted, but now cannot leave even if she yearns to. There doesn't seem to be a tissue anywhere. Alison rummages in her bag but produces only a make-up purse and mirror into which she looks wildly, watching herself cry.

Tess trots off to get some tissues from the upstairs bathroom, ascending the galaxy of posters, their endless allure falling on dulled eyes. That is the stairwell where Grizelda fell, pushed by a friend, the one with the big dark eyes, so Alison told her. Why had Grizelda chosen friends like that at school? Was the absence of the father so very dire?

A resounding click and bang echoes through the bathroom

window. It is the noise of the double-doors swinging open in the courtyard to let someone in.

Grizelda must be home at last. Back at last, her footsteps echoing loud and un-ghostlike on the gravel, inconsiderate as a cat on heat. It seems Alison can milk suffering out of anything, even a night on the tiles; such a traditional adolescent rebellion.

Tess moves downstairs again, holding a box of tissues, and through the stairwell sees Alison peering through her front door, waiting to see her bad daughter walk up the outside staircase, messy and defiant.

But no, the footsteps continue on past her entrance and through into the apartment of the Americans below; someone returning probably from a nightclub.

Alison shrinks back into her flat, into herself; slumps on the floor. Has she fainted? But no, she has started to scrawl something on the walls, graffiti on her own walls, scrawling something with a tube of lipstick. She is writing words. Paul's name, perhaps, over and over, or Grizelda's, or is it just the hieroglyphs of despair?

She might as well be smearing shit, for there seems no meaning to it as far as Tess can tell. Alison sits there slumped and swaying, humming a ditty, scrawling away.

Then Tess gets angry. Angrier than she has ever been in her life; angrier than when she woke, bruised, in a room of broken bottles.

A huge spurt of lava erupts; lava bursting all the more violently because of the pressure that has built up for so long.

Loss skims the creamiest life, fades the colours, saps the apples and flowers. Loss on a grand scale makes loss a familiar smell, a home smell; loss turned Grizelda on.

She was sick of all the stinking loss. The veil of tears. The loss in the mother's milk. And sick of being silent, of being first her mother's, then Paul's liegeman, sick of probity, rectitude, decorum, tight lips. And sick of *ssshhh*. Sick of covering up for others; sick of mopping up; looking after Mother between lovers, getting rid of lovers who had become a nuisance; writing those letters that became a little mechanical over the years. Dear Raoul, Philippe, Joseph: fuck off. They must have been somewhat humiliated if they recognized her handwriting.

What good had it done, all this deception, all this grief? She could make it vanish, *pouf!* Make it go away. Cleanse the house. Exorcize the dead room upstairs where his black coat still hangs so meaningfully over the back of his swing chair. She could throw the bloody coat over the sleeping *clochard* outside. Yes, she could take it over the road in the shivering dawn light and put it over the chap on the air vent outside the Deaf and Dumb Institute. He would wake to find himself covered in cashmere and astrakhan and believe in miracles. She looked down the stairwell at her insane hostess, smearing her own walls with shit.

She had the power to tear all that grief out of her. Tear it out by the roots. Then Alison could substitute anger for grief. Anger has more torque. It's pugilistic. Once you know you have nothing to grieve for. Once you know there was no bloody loss. Once you know Paul had already left you. Definitely. Before he died.

After the shock you might have a chance to live. Grizelda would be free of her sad enchantment if she knew she would just have been another child of divorced parents; the most common of situations now, in 1993. There were more kids like that in every school than children of mythically happy couples. Where then would be the high tragedy?

She opened her mouth to scream out the truth. The words so long swallowed are ready to leap out; flame from her fire-eater's mouth. She can feel the fire scorching her throat, feeling it burning her insides. She opens her mouth, to solve it, to scream out flames and fire and brimstone, to boil up the world.

'*Bbbrrrrr. Bbrrrrrrr.*'

The madwoman below springs up and rushes into the salon to answer the phone as if it were a fire alarm. Tess plods down the stairs, holding the box of tissues which she has strangled, nearly dismembered. She stands next to Alison in the *salon*, a sentry, ready for a fainting fit; bad news about Grizelda, the police on the line; disaster. They shouldn't let her into their lives. She is the harbinger of disaster.

'Yes. Yes. What?' The wretched dog has woken and is barking inanely. Alison puts one hand over her ear and concentrates.

'Ah yes. Yes. She's here.' She hands Tess the telephone, puzzled. 'It's for you, my dear.'

It is four in the morning. Everything always happens to her at dawn in Paris. She stares for a moment at the aching light on the Deaf and Dumb garden and reaches out for the receiver.

'Hullo. Oh. Dear God . . . *Mother!*'

Mother has already phoned Tess's hotel in the rue du Louvre and they gave her this number. (Tess always has to leave her number in case a buyer wants to place an order.) But of course at this time it is sure to be no one but Mother. Mother in a state. Unmindful of the time. Typically self-absorbed, wanting to talk about her latest affair. No difference to her if it is four in the morning or four in the evening. Her egotism is endearing in a way, if you don't bear the brunt of it. Every time is confession time. And hasn't her daughter always been the repository of her triumphs and humiliations?

Tess covers the receiver and hisses. 'Just Mother. Sorry . . . ' And she rolls her eyes ceilingwards.

## Alison 1993

Alison raises her eyebrows; rendered sane by the sudden interruption, like a slap in the face.

She lies down on the yellow sofa and closes her eyes while Tess stands there (leaning against the wall after a while) and listens, has to listen, has to let her talk herself down, talk it away, but she doesn't get the whole story, of course. The same old story; new every time.

While she listens her concentration wavers. At one point she has a sudden image of her mother's past; her mother as a child before the war, escaping across Europe with an aunt.

*The child (her mother) is sleeping in a second-class carriage. At the border a soldier turns on the light and begins searching. He points to a large square box on the luggage rack. What is this object? What does it contain? This is the perfect vehicle for smuggling. If, as the aunt claims, it is a musical instrument for the child, let the child prove it. The soldier wakes her and drags her on to the platform. In the interrogation hut he orders her to play the accordion. The child that was her mother, shivering in her night-dress, fingers stiff with fear, whimpers. But she does it. She plays 'Bagatelle', a message of cheer in the wasteland. One guard waltzes with his rifle. Another gives her a sweet.*

'Of course I'm listening, Mother. What happened next? Go on, get it all out of your system.'

# TWENTY

Tess puts down the telephone.

'What was all that about?' Alison is rather annoyed, peering up at her from her sofa.

'Silly old bat. What is she? She's nearly a fucking septuagenarian! Her latest obsession is 40. Until tonight he's been too kind to mention her age. She's been hurling herself at him like a cat at the moon.'

Tess stalks out of the room into the hallway, leaving the door flung wide. In one swift lunge she rips down the poster of Humphrey Bogart. The rage that had been on the point of eruption when the telephone rang shoots on to the movie stars. She carries on up the stairs, ripping them to pieces: Jean Gabin. Michèle Morgan in her bloody raincoat. Gérard Philipe with the dancing eyes. Why do they always have to see the world through a veil of smoke? Why does it always have to be raining? Why is there so much fog? Why doesn't anything ever happen in the sunlight? She blames them all, blames them for everything.

She is panting. Alison is following behind her, laughing, quietly at first, then louder and louder. Mad, infectious mirth. She begins laughing too, sitting down helplessly in the white drifts of paper that blow in the draught of

175

the stairwell; Jean Gabin's mouth; Alain Delon's eyes; the hands of Bogey and cigarette smoke, cigarette smoke every-where; rolling them, lighting them, inhaling and exhaling them, it made their shallowness look so deep. Bits of the day before yesterday's glamour float in the air like snow.

Alison clutches the banisters, bent double with laughter. The helpless laughter of the fatigued.

Grizelda is standing at the door, watching them, amazed. She is used to coming home to her mother in tears; always in tears, looking up at her through parted fingers, saying, 'You look like something the cat dragged in.'

But now, it seems, Grizelda feels annoyed. There is an anti-climax involved here. Mother is with a friend in a pile of torn-up posters and they are in fits of giggles like kids after a pillow-fight in the dorm. While she has been out there. Out there on the darkling plain (Dad's favourite poem, or so Mum says), where ignorant armies clash by night. And here they are in the middle of their fragile, well-lit crucible of fine objects and glowing colours, laughing cosily like two women folding sheets in a Dutch Interior painting, as if the world isn't full of rubble and wrecked planes and shit.

'Hullo, darling,' her mother says, hiccuping a little from her laughing fit. 'This is Tess Deutch, your old babysitter from the days of yore.' They roar with laughter again. It's getting more annoying.

'Have you two been up all night?' Grizelda asks in a tight, disapproving voice; then goes off, scowling, into the kitchen, from where they hear her shout, 'There's no more coffee!' Furious with them, stealing her thunder; up to their own tricks.

'There are some croissants from yesterday. Just need heating up,' responds Alison with maddening cheer.

Tess watches the little non-drama, not oblivious of the scars on the child's neck. Has someone tried to strangle her? Does she really need to sail so close to the wind?

Grizelda joins them in the *salon* with a tray of tea and croissants. Tess has drunk so much caffeine she will not sleep properly for days. Alison begins a series of huge, naked yawns. Then staggers out of the room.

Grizelda looks at Tess with hatred. 'I suppose you've been going down Memory Lane?'

'It's a long lane. I first came to Paris with my mother and she used to drag me off to the *marché aux puces*, and I suppose I fell in love with the place way back then.'

Grizelda crashes her cup on the floor, spilling a puddle of tea. 'You make me sick. You sit there goofing on about Paris and the flea market. Can't you see the whole city is one enormous flea market? You just happen to stay around the posh bits where the fleas are gilded and the junk costs a bomb, where they wait like spiders for loaded American tourists. You should leave the Left Bank and the flea market and all those corny old spots and look at the underbelly; the periphery; the twentieth *arrondisse-ment*; what's happening now. You don't know Paris. It's about to burst at the seams with all the underdogs pushing it apart.'

Grizelda's face is red. She is leaning so far forward her sleeve is dipping into the remains of her tea.

'It's the newspapers,' Tess soothes, still the babysitter, 'you get to believe that horror is all there is. You forget that almost anyone, with a few bob, can come here and be in a place which, visually, is the perfect city.'

'Visually, visually, visually *shit*.' Grizelda wrings out her sleeve. Her face switches off. From mean to blank.

Tess knows she thinks her a fool; can't recover from a

schoolgirl crush: Paris by the Seine, Paris in the Luxembourg Gardens, Paris in the Furstenberg square by moonlight. But it wasn't just that, it was more subtle than that. It was the way the napkins were folded. It was French civilization in the fold of a napkin. Hers might be the last generation to remember it, the last repository of that precious knowledge . . . But, yes, Grizelda is also right, her adolescent crush has a vice-like grip on the heart.

Where is Alison? Has she passed out upstairs? She'd better let herself out of here. Quickly.

'How did you meet my father?' Grizelda looks at her accusingly.

Tess sits back in the chair. No use sulking with the brat; the once-silken baby-skin on her neck bruised by the underdog city.

'I first saw him in a bar. Then we ran into each other in the market in rue Mouffetard. I was buying cheese. He asked me to babysit soon after that. It was a miracle. A regular job. I could stay on in Paris, you see.'

'For how long exactly did you stay on?'

'Exactly?' She closes her eyes and thinks. 'Eight months.'

'For eight months you saw my father nearly every day?' Grizelda looks at Tess with eyes glinting with something that must be envy.

Grizelda puts down her cup again, more gently this time; gets up and begins pacing the room, coming to rest in front of a painting of violets that has been in that spot since Paul's time. With her back turned, she says, 'What was he like? With me?'

There is a familiar honking noise starting up from the Deaf and Dumb garden as if from a flight of migrating birds. The early-rising children have been let out to play before breakfast and are throwing balls around with loud, voiceless cries; whether of anger, spite, triumph or delight it is impossible to interpret. It's harsher than an owl's cry but with the same eeriness.

'Your father used to sit you on his knee and brush your hair. He used to watch those deaf and dumb children playing out there; listen to their cries.'

'He used to brush my hair?' Her head tilts back as she speaks, her back moves like a stretching cat.

'It was the one thing that soothed you.'

'Was it?'

The voice is very small now.

'Ah yes. You revelled in it. Sitting in that chair there.'

Grizelda moves over and sits down on that same Victorian chair, re-covered a few times since then, of course.

'He used to watch the garden and brush your hair, waiting for me to arrive; to take over before they went off to their Embassy parties. He was very gentle with you. Too gentle. He took infuriating ages doing up your buttons.'

'He used to sit just here, the way I'm sitting? Where would he be looking?'

'Over there.' Tess points to a spot beyond the willow near the fountain where the last wolf-child in France used to sit rocking quietly to himself, baying at the moon.

'Tell me more, everything you can think of. Everything he said . . . did.'

Avoiding his photograph, his quizzical laugh, she dredges up scraps of domestic detail: his ineptitude with nappies; his compulsion to purchase his baby expensive dresses which were always too big; his ability to make her burp when everyone else had failed.

Alison emerged in her red dressing gown. 'I'm going to try to get a little sleep. Grizelda, will you take Puffy for his morning walk?'

They all look at Puffy, but he is snoozing again in his

basket. No point in disturbing the beast. And Tess must go now. This minute.

In the hall she puts on her coat, picks up the huge shoulderbag with its secret contents of broken umbrella and newspaper.

Grizelda gives her a white rose, one of those Tess had brought for Alison last night, a century ago. She twists it through her lapel. The scent, less adorable, is of cigarettes and endurance. Grizelda smells of garlic and sex; smells of the Métro; a smell Tess likes. Her rebellious stench is wasted on an old francophile.

Alison considers her for a moment with a full gaze. 'And take care with the small print on your contract. I suppose you speak good French now.'

'I never did get around to that advanced course at the Institut Français, I'm afraid.'

'You disappeared, didn't you. Well, don't disappear on us again.'

They wave, giving each other the goodbye look, belying their words. The mother and daughter see a smart woman of desirable age but somehow muted, not quite vivid enough for the risks life requires. And she absorbs what she knows will be her last sight of Alison: Alison dignified by sadness; and the rat-tailed daughter, angry as hell.

She has no idea if Grizelda will survive her walks on the wild side. But she will always have to hold in the truth like the fire-eater; let it scorch her guts; never spit out those tongues of flame. Although it might be a good, cleansing thing to do in the long run, God knows.

And it might not.

Perhaps it would be the end of them.

She walks away in the struggling sunlight, her shadow following her along the wall. On the corner she pauses by the familiar plaque:

## Alison 1993

*Ici est tombé*
*Gerald Martinet*
*2 août, 1944*
*Fusillé par les allemands*
*à l'age de 28*

She counts the bullet holes. It had taken seven bullets to kill him. He had been young, too young to die, leaving behind the usual tangle of grieving women. Love in all its guises. She takes the rose from her lapel and places it below the plaque. She moves off across the Luxembourg Gardens, dropping the broken umbrella in a bin, but keeping the newspaper dated 1974, with its headline about a plane crash in a field of lavender.

The first tramps are setting up their day camps, appropriately under the Dionysus figure. She thinks of Paul waving his last goodbye through the back window of the taxi. That trust, the nearest she ever got to his love. And for the first time wonders what he meant by his 'ssshhh'. Why did she have to be quiet at that stage of the game? She could have ridden into the Count's house on a charger, galloped up the stairs and smashed the door down to leave his letter by the bloody clock. He had gone by then anyway. He was unreachable. He had *foutu le camp*. But no, he wasn't gone, not quite. It was essential that she didn't arouse suspicion for another few hours, enough time for him to get safely on that plane. He had only meant her silence to last for an hour or two before his *fait* was *accompli*.

It was going to have to last for ever.

Should she drop in on the café? There will be a new generation of Stellas and Francines and Yugoslavs. Or have the same old ex-pats and drifters stayed on, become fixtures? Was that a failure to mature? Was there something wrong with them, blighted at the roots? Would they always be the lurchers in the shadows; the rustics with straw in their hair peering into the windows of stiff French dinner parties where the cheese is brought to table like a national monument?

Never mind. Certain places, like Paris, have something for everyone. They are God's apology for their upbringing; still seductive after all these years, whatever the long, withdrawing roar of the *fin de siècle*.

But tonight she would return to where she belongs. Designing droll knitwear, avoiding chaos and the darkling plain where aeroplanes crash on their way to the sun.

Now, though, she will go straight ahead to the river and walk along the embankment on the other side to the Grand Palais, stopping to watch the anglers in the spring light, and consider the day; her last day in Paris. Stupid to waste it in sleep.